SAM'S MIND WAS MUSH.

The drug had done its work. Now he stood before the open window and looked down through the gloom to the street.

The stranger was repeating: "You will jump now."

His eyes still fastened on the pavement below, Durell heard himself saying, "NOOooo . . . ," and half-turned back into the room. The word seemed to last an hour. A day. Suns came and went. Comets flashed.

The universe exploded—a shot rang out.

Durell swayed, looking back into the room.

A golden-haired woman stood over the stranger's body.

"You killed him," Sam said groggily.

"Of course. And you almost took a seven-story step out that window."

"Who are you?" he asked.

"Why, darling," she said, "I'm your wife."

Assignment 13th Princess

Will B. Aarons

FAWCETT GOLD MEDAL • NEW YORK

ASSIGNMENT 13TH PRINCESS

ISBN 0–449–13919–0

Printed in the United States of America

10 9 8 7 6 5 4 3 2

Chapter 1

Durell thought he must be dreaming.

"To the window, please."

"The—window?" Durell stared at the olive-skinned man through lusterless eyes.

"There's a good fellow."

The man's voice came softly as the hiss of a snake; a sound of arrow feathers; the purr of a razor through silk. Durell could not accept that the sound was yellow, the words coming out like sulphur smoke.

He would wake up and it would be all right, he told himself.

The color of the words mingled and merged into the hair of a dimly remembered freckle-faced blonde who had sat beside him on the airplane, and his dream became mixed like the colors of oil on water. Something deep in his mind wondered about that girl. He did not know if there was a connection between her and this tormentor.

Somewhere in the roots of Durell's consciousness the will to live struggled against blind obedience—and he found himself moving tentatively, crabwise, toward the open window. His feet weighed a thousand pounds, but his head floated ethereally without weight or substance. He was aware of his surroundings, but as from a distance, vaguely, a disembodied shade in a fog through which came neither feeling nor reason.

But he would awaken, and it would end.

The man gestured impatiently with a Beretta automatic that was aimed at Durell's chest. Durell had no fear of the gun.

Nor of the open window, seven stories above a London street.

Not even of the note he had compliantly written, which stated simply: "I can't go on."

Ordinarily Durell saw himself as a small cog in the machinery that kept the earth turning a spin or two ahead of the madmen and zealots whose schemes could leave it a nuclear cinder. Training and retraining at the Farm operated by K Section in the Maryland countryside and more years than he cared to think about in the shadow land of international intrigue had prepared him for self-sacrifice.

But now he was a vital cog.

If he died in this sedate Oxford Street hotel room, the Western world literally could spin to a halt. Commerce and industry might wither, cities die. Nations would lie enfeebled, an invitation to the conqueror's rape and sword.

All because of greed and parochial politics.

Because of oil.

Such thoughts now were melted like lead filings in his chemical-numbed brain, run together in a solid lump that his reasoning could not digest.

The breeze that blew through the window chilled the room even though it was summer. The window was big in its old-fashioned, beige-painted frame and fully opened to the late-afternoon sky. Durell saw the view with abrupt clarity, as in a perfectly focused snapshot. Sporadic rain-showers had littered diamond beads of water across the sill and darkened the carpet with moisture. Beyond the umber drapes oozy clouds whirled a shattered puzzle across the heavens. The weak, filtered sunlight glazed high-rise windows with pewter and deepened the gray of weathered Portland stone and turned bricks to blood. Treetops tossed in Grosvenor Square, site of the American embassy, and the mist blew against St. Paul's burnished dome and the spires of Parliament in the distance.

Durell wanted to go no closer.

But something said go ahead. Make it easy. It's only a dream.

You can't stop a dream.

His gaze turned dully toward the gun muzzle and then the man's face, a viper's visage of long, broad nose and bright, black eyes, and he felt a disquieting affinity for him. After all, they both were professionals.

The man's loose, alert stance; the relaxed but ready manner in which he held his weapon; even the mask of his sinister smile—all bespoke a calm competence that only training and experience could buy. He might have been a stockbroker in his expensive pinstripe suit and vest. He wore a pale yellow tie with a tastefully muted pattern of woven silk flowers. The flowers blossomed larger, coming alive under Durell's dreamlike vision. He saw a gold band set with a pink pearl that shone on the little finger of the man's left hand.

Over the smell of carpet shampoo and fresh linens came the scents of oak leaves from Hyde Park and rain and automobile exhaust, all mixed and meaningless.

Durell was aware of the cool breeze from the window as it blew directly on his back now, the muted rumble of vehicles coming from a great distance. Without concept of time his mind wandered through a torturous labyrinth of thought and dwelt on space.

He had come far to meet the Israelis.

Where were they?

Was this man one of them? he thought absurdly. Anger pinched him through the befuddled layers of his dream. He wanted to speak, but the concepts would not come together. He decided he would discover what he had wanted to say when he awakened. Meanwhile this man would lead him through the nightmare, tell him what to do. He must rely on him. Submit.

He felt each second as it slipped away in a tenuous drool.

He did not know how long ago the man had ordered him to the window, but now his tapered gambler's fingers rested lightly on its damp sill, and the traffic noise took on a regular beat in rhythm with his heart. The beat increased in tempo and volume as he looked down, down, his eyes seeming to fall through the air, and saw red double-decker buses and tiny MGs, motorbikes and

Bentleys crowding the streets of fashionable Mayfair seven stories below.

Then his flat, lifeless eyes turned back over his shoulder toward the man.

The man's grin showed a great spread of flashing fire.

Yellow words came out of the fire:

"Quickly, now. Jump!"

Lights had burned most of the previous night in the executive wing of the White House, the Pentagon, and the gray stone Georgian house at No. 20 Annapolis Street that was headquarters for K Section, trouble-shooting arm of the CIA.

The ring of a telephone had awakened Durell at 3:41 A.M.

"You'll be traveling, Sam," he had been told. But not where. Or why.

He had not taken time to brew the chicory-laced Louisiana coffee with which he preferred to greet the day. He had shaved quickly, thrown a few things into a suitcase. Twenty minutes later a motor-pool driver in a black government Chevrolet had picked him up at his apartment, located in a red-brick, marble-trimmed building on a shady street near Rock Creek Park.

General Dickinson McFee, the small, gray chief of K Section, sat rigidly behind his desk, shoulders squared. He seemed never to relax, Durell thought.

"The old emir of Dhubar, Sheik Yusuf, bought it last night, Samuel. Like a bolt out of nowhere. Assassinated. The country's going crazy."

"Who's behind it, sir?"

"We don't know—but that isn't our first concern. You've heard of the Thirteenth Princess?"

Durell nodded. "Princess Ayla—descendant of the Ottoman Turks—wife of Sheik Zeid. He'll be ascending his father's throne."

"He may keep it if he's lucky. Mobs are roaming the streets, demanding his wife's head—you know how the Arabs hated the Turks under the Ottoman Empire."

"They didn't complain when Sheik Zeid married her."

McFee's slight flip of the hand was disparaging. "He

was just a playboy, Sam. They had given up caring what he did. But now he's their ruler. We may be able to put a cap on this thing before it blows sky high, but it means getting Princess Ayla out of there until Sheik Zeid can put his house in order."

Durell spoke quietly. "You think the same people who engineered the assassination are using her presence to keep the civil disturbances going?"

"I have little doubt of it—they're keeping the mobs at a fury pitch."

"She may not wish to go."

"That could be a problem. But you will convince her."

"There must be others better suited to coddle a princess. Why me?"

"You're a friend of her mother, the former Nadine Carroll?"

"Friendship of a sort that goes only so far, sir." Durell's tone was dubious.

"Oh?" McFee lifted a gray brow. "The lady seems to think you would go all the way for her. She sent for you. She says her husband, Prince Tahir, and Sheik Zeid have refused her pleas to send Princess Ayla out of danger. Zeid loves his wife too much to be without her, the mother says, and God only knows why Tahir would expose Ayla to such threats."

"I'd say Prince Tahir doesn't care to risk her not returning to Dhubar. Any throne for her would be better than none in his view."

"In any case, you're the only one who will do, Samuel. The mother will help you, intercede for you with her daughter, pave the way. But you have to get her out on your own." McFee bent forward, an angular little man in a light gray suit and charcoal tie. Durell noted with discomfort that his blackthorn walking stick leaned against his desk. It was lethal with a dozen hidden gimmicks dreamed up by the lab boys. "Keep in mind," McFee continued, "that if the radicals take over, they could turn off the spigot of the world's sixth largest oil producer at any whim—the use of oil for political black-mail would rise to unprecedented and intolerable levels."

"You'd think Princess Ayla would be more than happy to take a holiday."

"She may be—or she may refuse to leave her husband. But the only chance of saving that country lies in getting her out of the spotlight and off the stage. Expect the radicals to try to prevent that—hatred of her is all that holds their brewing street revolution together. But get her out, Sam." McFee's voice was severe. "Get her out any way it takes."

Durell gave a grim thought to his chances. "I'll do what I can, sir."

"One thing: don't let Sheik Zeid catch you at it. He'll never forgive. We will lose either way."

Durell breakfasted on bacon and eggs in the final moments before his flight was announced over the public address system at Dulles International Airport. Servicemen, sharply attired businessmen, entertainers in unlikely getups, each seeming purposeful and aloof, converged on the gate of the London-bound BOAC 747.

More out of habit than necessity here, Durell regarded them all with suspicion.

Beyond the window of the restaurant the morning had turned hot and muggy, the woods and fields hazed with a bright humidity. He did not care to think what the climate had to offer in Dhubar on the sizzling Persian Gulf.

His practiced eye swept the faces of passengers as they joined him in first class, then floated briefly over the girl seated next to him. She might have looked callow with her sunny blond hair and faint facial dusting of copper freckles, but something in her hazel eyes said she had seen too much for that. Her carriage of straight back, high bust, and long, elegant legs was almost military. She was tall, at least five feet ten. Her slender height conveyed the delicacy of a column of smoke on a breathless morning, but Durell decided that impression was not to be trusted. There was a cool self-assurance in her stylishly understated costume: denim slacks, copper-buttoned denim safari jacket, red scarf tucked into her pale blue collar, and a pink beret.

"I feel like we're old friends," she said and smiled.

"Do you?" A prompt apprehension crossed Durell's mind. The opposition in his business could come in any form—a child, a dwarf, a beautiful woman.

She ignored his tone. "Let's pretend we are, anyway. Shall we?"

"What's your name?"

"Dara. Dara Allon."

It rang no bells, sounded no alarms. She wore a wedding ring. She did not ask his name.

Durell rolled onto his shoulder, his nostrils sweetened by her summery cologne, and gazed across the empty sky. He would try to ignore her, he decided. As chief field agent for K Section he long ago had narrowed the circle of those he trusted almost to the vanishing point. He had become accustomed to a solitary life spent grappling with danger and the unknown.

The wrong word to a stranger, he had learned, could be as deadly as a bullet.

He turned his mind to the Thirteenth Princess, remembered that she had been an embarrassment to the old emir. Nowhere had hatred for the Ottoman Turks been as visceral as among the fiercely proud Arabs, who, from Baghdad to Cairo, had been under the yoke of Istanbul for hundreds of years. And Princess Ayla was descended from the very sultans who had so despotically ruled them.

The Turks had lost their empire in World War I, and that humiliation, plus the Turkish people's resentment of the threatened dismemberment of their Anatolian homeland, had led to civil war and the proclamation of a republic. Durell recalled that the last Ottoman sultan, Mehmed VI Vahideddin, thirty-sixth sultan of the line, had been ousted in 1922. He stole out of Istanbul aboard a British battleship bound for San Remo. The Ottoman ruling family was expelled in its entirety two years later.

Prince Tahir was born into one of its branches that very year. He became a shrewd and ruthless businessman and multiplied a tidy inheritance into a sprawling fortune. He had an affinity with the international set, favored the Riviera, Rio, and *chemin de fer*. He married film actress Nadine Carroll, known to Hollywood as the Platinum

Brat. To the best of Durell's knowledge, she had made an excellent wife and mother.

Princess Ayla's childhood had been one of quiet, sheltering luxury such as only the very rich can afford and only nobility can command. Before the child was grown, she had seen most of the world from the most exclusive vantage points.

She had been raised to be a queen.

Durell guessed that Prince Tahir must have spent sleepless nights as he quested for the domain he wanted her to have. And now she was Princess of Dhubar. Surly and headstrong, Tahir would not be pleased if she stepped aside now, even temporarily.

Sheik Zeid had been reared in the tradition of desert warriors, then schooled at Yale, Durell's alma mater. He could pilot a Phantom or recite *Leaves of Grass* with equal ease. He had gravitated away from the old Moslem ways and joined the Grand Prix racing crowd and lavished his money on formula cars and glamorous women. He had married perhaps the most glamorous of the lot, with her royal blood and oriental beauty: Princess Ayla.

The Arabs of Dhubar disdained to have her Turkish name in their mouths. She was the thirteenth child born to the Turkish royal line since the family's expulsion, and to them she would remain the Thirteenth Princess.

Last month, in London, she had given birth to Sheik Zeid's first son, the new crown prince. Now there was Ottoman blood in the succession to the throne.

The populace of Dhubar had just exploded in a frenzy, and all its anger and suspicion over the brutal slaying of the old emir had been focused on Princess Ayla. Someone was using the event to engineer a power play against her husband, the best sources said.

"An insider is orchestrating it, mark my word," McFee had said, "someone the radicals have touched with money or the lure of power."

One thing about the situation, Durell thought as he declined coffee from the stewardess: it had taken guts for the Thirteenth Princess to return to Dhubar. To stay there after the riots of last night simply was reckless, unless she had no choice.

In which case his job would be all the harder.

The 747 settled over the green geometry of the English countryside and bumped down at Heathrow Airport twenty miles from central London.

The blonde, who was nearer the aisle, arose first, and Durell became aware that the movement of deplaning passengers had halted. He looked up. Dara Allon stood straight and tall in the aisle, arms crossed beneath her breasts, feet planted in a wide stance. She did not move. Those behind her waited politely, suitbags over shoulders, small valises and packages resting on chair arms. Cool air thrummed through the ducts of the airplane, but the passengers looked hot and harried. They stared at him. Dara smiled, beckoned him into the aisle.

"After you," he said, in hopes of dismissing her.

"I won't hear of it." Her smile was determined.

Durell's thank-you was somewhat irritable. Going down the aisle, the skin at the nape of his neck started to tingle. He did not like her back there behind him, he realized. Not at all.

She stuck close, too close, a beautiful, summery-scented, strangely steely presence, but he broke out of line, moved fast, and gave her the slip in the crowd going through customs.

The drizzling sky above the ultramodern terminal building wheeled with gulls, and a faint sharpness of salt water braced the air. Bright green coaches of the London Country Bus Service were parked nearby.

He looked right and left. No one seemed to await him.

Then he saw her again, now in enormous dark glasses despite the soggy weather. Her head jerked in recognition, short, yellow hair swaying across a cheek, and she took a step in his direction. He buried himself in a crowd demanding taxis, pushed to the curb and ordered a driver to take him to the Hertford Hotel on Oxford Street. A glance through the rear window showed Dara's dismayed face as she watched his departing cab.

She might have wished only for a date—or for his head on a platter.

In his business, Durell could never tell.

His cab rolled through dreary suburbs on a flood of noisy traffic. He could not be certain about the vehicles that clogged the street behind but saw nothing to allay or intensify suspicion. Still, he had a sense of being followed. Maybe it was only the girl and her strange behavior that were on his mind. He had a hunch she was like cloth of fine silk—folded around a sword.

He could not see that he was followed, but he switched from the taxi to the Underground, just in case. An enormous escalator fed him down beneath the street, where he bought a ticket from a vending machine. None of the other riders caught his eye. They were just faces. He left the Tube at Marble Arch, surrendered his punched ticket, and took the lift to the street. Not far down Park Lane was Speaker's Corner, where anyone could speak—and be jeered—on any subject. It was in the Knightsbridge angle of Hyde Park, once a favorite hunting ground of Henry VIII.

Durell hoped no one hunted him.

The mist had turned to rain. Londoners under black umbrellas swarmed like beetles. Durell stood under an awning before a pub. The plate glass window of a turf accountant's office showed the street back to him. He scented greasy fish and chips as a stringy-haired youth strode by munching out of a brown paper bag. The afternoon was gloomy, the city dreary.

He hailed another taxi.

All he knew of the next phase of his assignment was that a room awaited him at the Hertford.

"The Israelis want their own close-up on the situation, Samuel," McFee had said. "They have no embassy in Dhubar, no base of operations. You'll provide cover for the penetration."

"I'd rather not."

"Seems the Israelis are calling in some debts."

Durell spoke bluntly. "It adds risk to my primary mission, sir."

"The Joint Chiefs called the shot—I just spoke with

the chairman. Sugar Cube is in their corner. You'll be contacted in London."

"You're giving me no choice?"

"It'll work out."

"I hope so. Any other chores? Errands? Odd jobs?" Durell felt his Cajun temper rising. "I work cheap."

"You'll have your hands full." McFee said it with a thin sound that might have been a chuckle, as if delivering a genteel punch line.

Durell wondered what the joke was.

The lobby of the Hertford was old and elegant, with scalloped marble pillars, ivory-painted walls, and white leather-upholstered furniture. The air was redolent of expensive tobacco and damp tweed. It was the sort of place that operated on a whisper and a nod. Durell signed the register, made a telephone call from a polished mahogany booth, ascended to his floor in a brass bird-cage lift. He momentarily studied the door to his room, saw no scratches or dents beside the knob, no evidence of forced entry. He palmed the handle, tried it gently. The door was properly locked. A twist of the key and he pushed the door open, reached in and around to press the light button, kept the door between him and the room. There was no explosion, no sound of surprise. He moved inside and tossed his suitcase on the green bedspread and briefly noted a vase of fresh red carnations. Methodically following procedure, he checked the bathroom and an enormous oak wardrobe, his .38 S. & W. loose in his grip.

Durell was a tall man, heavily muscled but surprisingly quick on his feet. He had dark blue eyes that could turn almost black. His face was lean and careful and hid his thoughts most of the time, so that those closest to him often wondered what went on under that cap of thick, black hair just touched with gray at the temples. Despite his height he had learned the tricks of losing himself in a crowd, but a trained observer would see by his bearing that he was honed to quick and deadly combat.

He could kill in many ways, with a finger, a pin, a rolled newspaper.

But he preferred the snub-nosed .38.

He paused in the middle of the large floral rug. This seemed just an ordinary room. His eyes slid to the white china vase with the carnations, and he considered it as he listened to the silence in the hall. He studied the flowers with deliberate care. There was no note. Then he turned away, checked table lamp and headboard, telephone, and ceiling lighting fixture for bugs.

Satisfied, he exhaled a slow breath, turned once more to the vase. He regarded it as too obvious to hide a listening device, but he could not afford to ignore it, so he bent over it and spread the blossoms.

There was a wicked spewing noise.

Something wet and acrid stung his eyes and nose.

Durell's throat made a harsh sound of disgust and rage as he stumbled back, wiping at his eyes. The vase crashed against the floor, spilling red flowers, and a small metal cylinder, stiff tripwire attached to its valve, rolled between his feet.

His struggle against the mind-warping, will-demolishing chemical was brief and vain. The world broke into pieces and spun around, flotsam in a whirlpool of incomprehension. The thump of his collapse to the floor came magnified a thousandfold and boomed in his ears like thunder.

He had no idea how much time went by.

Then he heard a door open. It did not bother him. A soft-edged voice told him to stand, and he did so—this was a dream, of course. Obeying without question, he held his arms out and watched calmly as the dapper, swarthy man fanned him, then kicked his fallen .38 out of the way.

And now Durell stood before the open window and looked down through the gloom and rain to where the dish-shaped street lamps stared back like a row of tiny eyes.

The man was repeating: "You will jump now."

Abruptly a vestigial will asserted itself. His eyes still fastened on the pavement below, Durell heard himself saying, "NOOooo . . . ," and half-turned back into the room. The word seemed to last an hour. A day. Suns came and went. Comets flashed.

The universe exploded—a shot rang out.

Durell swayed, looking back into the room.

The golden-haired Dara stood stiffly over the man's body, narrow lips drawn taut at the corners. A wisp of oil smoke rose from a Colt over-and-under derringer she held by her thigh. Her hazel eyes glinted angrily beneath their sweep of lashes as she glanced at her victim, then back at Durell. She tossed a wing of hair away from her freckled cheek and calmly broke open the derringer and extracted a bright, hot cartridge.

"You don't look so well," she said.

Durell collapsed.

When he came to, nothing was changed in the room. The body still lay on the flowered rug where it had fallen among scattered red carnations and shards of the vase. His head was on Dara's knees. He could breathe more freely now; the world was real, tangible—the dream was over. He rubbed his eyes, stared up at the girl's solicitous face.

"You killed him," he said groggily.

"Of course. And you almost took a seven-story step out that window."

"Who are you?" he asked.

"Why, darling," she said, "I'm your wife."

Chapter 2

Durell sat up, shook his head, cleared the cobwebs. "No one mentioned a wife," he said.

"It's the cover we Israelis have established. Rather good, don't you think?"

"Does that explain the wedding ring?"

She held the smallish circle up to the light. "Not exactly every girl's dream, is it?"

"They picked what I could afford," Durell said. He twisted over to hands and knees. He felt a bit light-headed, but there seemed to be no other aftereffects of the drug.

"To make the story convincing, I had to come from America with you, of course," Dara said.

"You could have let me in on the gag."

"I wish now I had. Maybe after all my efforts you wouldn't have ditched me at the airport—is that the way you treat all the girls who show an interest in you? Anyway, I was afraid I would be overheard. It seemed safe enough to let the matter wait until we arrived in London."

Durell stood up, somewhat unsteadily, and rubbed his temples with the tips of his fingers.

"Are you all right?" Dara asked.

"I think so."

"He must have known about you, but not me."

"Your people reserved the room."

"He didn't break our security, Sam;"—it was the first time she had used his name, and there was a corner-of-the-mouth toughness to the way she spoke it—"otherwise he'd be alive, and we'd both be dead."

They stared at each other, now tense and angry. Rain blew in the open window. Durell closed it, pulled the curtains, scooped up his pistol, and pushed it into his waistband. He tried to put this poor beginning out of his mind—it was no surprise that he had been betrayed. That was part of his business. Things didn't change just because K Section's computer printout put his survival factor only a shade above zero. At KGB headquarters in Moscow, at No. 2 Dzherzhinsky Square, his dossier was marked with a red tab. He was also on the kill list in the files of the Peacock Branch of the Black House in Peking. The threat of death was with him always, in shadowed streets and dark wildernesses. He did not brood on it; that would only impair his functioning and invite disaster.

The drapes muffled the rattle of rain as Durell gazed at the corpse. "Any idea who he is?"

"They're all Arabs, aren't they?"

"Maybe in your world."

"London's a regular battleground since they've invested so enormously here," she said. "They own seven and a half billion dollars just in British government stocks, treasury bills, and sterling deposits. Our bureau has settled in side by side to gather what intelligence we can." She paused, blew an exasperated breath, and added, "Naturally, the Arabs resent us."

"Naturally," Durell said.

Hurriedly, he patted a wallet from the man's coat. Dara's derringer had drilled it, but enough was left of an international driver's license to identify the owner as George Allen Cucera, thirty-two, with an address in Thaxted, an old Saxon town about forty miles north of London. Durell had little doubt that the name and address were fakes. In any case, there was no time to go and see. Tomorrow he must be in Dhubar.

He pocketed the driver's license, nodded toward the body. "Let's get rid of it," he said. He grasped the wrists. "Help me straighten it. We'll roll it up in the carpet and dispose of both. There's an incinerator in the basement. I pulled the hotel plan from our files before leaving."

"Clever."

"Just cautious."

She tucked her derringer into her blouse and took the ankles, and they pulled the sacklike weight into a straight line, its head swinging down loosely, mouth open. A dark line of blood ran from the lips back to the ear. Dara showed no emotion as they rolled the remains in the rug and lugged it, via the freight elevator, to the basement incinerator. Most maintenance personnel were off duty now. They encountered no one. The oil-fired incinerator crackled, hissed, and blew as they headed back upstairs.

Durell dug a flask of bourbon from his suitcase and poured them drinks. He noted that his hand shook slightly and was annoyed. The warmth of the liquor glowed on

Dara's freckled cheeks as she sat on the green bedspread, legs curled under her, denims tight around her slender thighs and hips. There was a look of rock candy in her hazel eyes. You could break your jaw on her, Durell thought.

He spoke evenly, holding his glass: "There will be others, you know."

"Let 'em come."

"It isn't a game."

Her voice was flat with sarcasm. "That dead Arab wouldn't think so."

Durell watched her. She was too flip for his taste. He wished he knew more about her. She squirmed a little under his gaze, and her eyes clouded uncertainly. She raised her glass. "To our partnership?" she said.

"While it lasts," he said.

Durell did not care for this arrangement, not at all. He preferred to work alone, at least with someone tried and true, like Willie Wells, the black Philadelphian ex-mercenary; or the burly, tenacious Greek, Mike Xanakias, who had been in anti-Nazi partisan; or Chet Clauson in Vienna, a top Central for K Section.

But Clauson had been killed, he reminded himself.

So many had been killed.

His stare returned to the sleek, lethal Israeli girl. Only time would tell whether she was an asset or a liability. He tossed down the rest of his drink, decided to make the best of it. "Get off your fanny and take me to meet your boss," he said.

"Sure thing, Şam." Now she sounded subordinate, for no reason he could fathom.

As they left the room, the image of flashing death's teeth came back to haunt him for a moment, and he suppressed a shudder. Dara seemed to notice and took his arm.

Anyone who saw them might have taken them for just another pair of newlyweds.

They hired a Ford and took Bond Street south to Picadilly. Dara pointed to Asprey and Company, jewelers

who had received such a volume of business from visiting
Arabs, she said, that the shop had opened outlets in
Oman, Abu Dhabi, and Qatar. They turned west, and
Durell decided the black and silver Rolls Royce back
there, barely identifiable in the late dusk, was tailing
them. They slid past the high-walled gardens of Bucking-
ham Palace, and he said nothing. The overcast had
hastened the night, and street lamps, neon over shops
and pubs and discos, the lights of cars, made a circus
of the street. Rain had become fine mist that wafted
glowing through the lights and made headlamps fall as
sheets of yellow silk on the pavement.

Durell caught the flick of Dara's eyes on the rear-
vision mirror. She did not mention the tail.

His familiarity with London was more than casual, but
she drove, handling the wheel with an alert expertise
that showed she would be at home in any metropolis.
She turned from Knightsbridge, with its elegant shops,
into Wilton Place and entered the Belgravia section south
of Hyde Park. A horse-drawn carriage clattered down a
cobbled back street, down a mews where once horses
were stabled and servants quartered. Now the mews
were inhabitated by fashionable painters and the owners
of trendy boutiques. It was a well-preserved neighborhood
of off-white Georgian and early Victorian town houses,
the dwellings of ambassadors, aristocrats, and wealthy
show people.

"An Arab spent a million dollars for that one," Dara
said, pointing through her reflection on the window. "He
is a sultan, of course. His people still live in woolen
tents."

"At least they have their Bedouin heritage. Wealthy
Texans were buying places here when all their neighbors
had were tumbledown shacks and outdoor privies."

Dara thrust out her jaw. "Whose side are you on?"

"It's not a matter of sides, just balance and perspective.
The Arabs aren't the first *nouveaux riches* to squander
their wealth."

"You want to talk about perspective, Sam? I'll tell you
about perspective." Dara's voice lowered. "Perspective is

what you get looking down the muzzle of a Syrian howitzer."

Durell regarded the woman, her grip tightening on the wheel. An unrelenting hatred seethed beneath that pretty exterior. He sighed, and said: "You're going to be a big hit in Dhubar."

As if venting her rage, Dara suddenly slammed her foot down on the gas pedal, and the slow-moving Ford screeched and roared around a corner into a dark street, rumbling over an old brick pavement. "Let's lose that Rolls," she cried happily.

"I was wondering if you ever would," Durell said, and twisted around to look through the rear window. A pair of headlamps, already two blocks distant and webbed with a misty glow, swung into the street after them.

Dara swung the wheel to the right, and the Ford fishtailed around a corner, burst out on Sloane Square near the Royal Court Theater, and barrelled down King's Road, weaving in and out of traffic. Dara handled the car better than most men in Durell's experience. Street moisture sizzled under the tires as she cut down to Cheyne Walk and came back up the Chelsea Embankment, with the Thames on their right glowing with buoys and ribbons of reflected light.

"They're out of sight; you've lost them," Durell said.

The car slowed. "Darn!" Dara said. "They didn't even make it interesting." She scanned the rear vision mirror with hopeful eyes, as if wishing that the shadowing car would appear again.

"Let's get on with our business," Durell said.

The house of the Israelis, brick with white stone trim, sat back from the street, behind a high privet hedge and cast-iron fence that gave it some protection against the curious and the deadly. The parlor was furnished with contemporary comfort and style, the walls paneled in dark wood. There were a hundred-year-old chandelier, books in the bookcases, a fire in the marble fireplace.

Beyond, every room in the house was coded to a purpose that allowed entry only by those assigned to it. Durell smelled hot electronic equipment as he strode along the upstairs hallway behind Dara. The girl walked with a purpose that did nothing to tether the womanly sway of her hips. Men came from behind doors with a prepossessed air, shirtsleeves rolled up. A glimpse inside one room gathered in a wicked little Uzi submachine gun that leaned against a wall.

The place was busy, taut, and efficient as a battle cruiser, everyone on a hair trigger.

Major Ethan Rabinovitch, chief of the unit, was a short, bulldoggish man with bitter brown eyes under shaggy brows. He embraced Dara like a father, and she hugged him back. Then they all sat down around the major's steel desk and talked above the muffled jangle of telephones, clack of typewriters and teletypes, a low hubbub of businesslike voices.

"What do you think of your new wife, Cajun?" the major asked.

"She can shoot and she can drive," Durell replied.

"You've already found out?"

Durell told him about the man in the Hertford and the car that had followed them from the hotel. He tossed the dead man's driver's license onto the major's desk.

"I'll have a man follow this up," Rabinovitch said, and dropped the card into his desk drawer. "My apologies for the rude reception. The Arab is getting frisky. Two letter bombs came yesterday. We'll have to move again, soon." He spoke matter-of-factly. "Any other problems?"

Durell looked at Dara, then answered the major's question. "I don't believe Miss Allon is suited to the job," he said bluntly. Dara went rigid and her thin, sharply defined lips opened to protest.

Rabinovitch cut her off with a wave of his meaty hand, narrowed his dark eyes at Durell: "Why?"

"She's too eager."

"We like that quality."

"My job isn't to kill Arabs, Major."

The major gave a grim smile. He started to say something, but seemed to change his mind. Then he said, "She comes highly recommended."

"By whom?"

"Me."

"And you've already arranged things with Washington, so there's no point in arguing it, right?" Durell felt the angry throb of his pulse.

Rabinovitch switched his gaze to Dara. In the pause that followed, they seemed to communicate with their eyes. Everything in this room, so unlike the comfortable front of the parlor downstairs, seemed made of ice and steel under the fluorescent lighting. Durell heard no street noises and judged the walls to have been fortified and braced, just in case a bomb should be left in a parked car nearby or a satchel charge should be thrown against the building. There were no windows in the room, although there must have been a row of blind openings in the outer wall in order to preserve the innocent appearance of the old town house.

Finally the major spoke: "We will maintain the present arrangement. It's too late to change, really."

"All right, Major," Durell rasped. "Have it your way. Just remember: I'm supposed to get Princess Ayla out of Dhubar with as few ripples as possible."

"Maybe you won't have to get her out," Major Rabinovitch replied. His bitter eyes seemed almost empty of light.

"What are you getting at?" Durell demanded. He did not like the feeling that was growing between his shoulders.

"Use your imagination."

"No, you tell me."

"There's nothing to tell." The major hunched his shoulders. "Just that stability in Dhubar is vital to Israel's national interest."

"And you would assassinate the princess to gain it."

"I didn't say that, Cajun."

"Don't even think it," Durell said, his voice low and even. He turned to Dara. "Understand?"

She smiled and widened her eyes. "Of course, Sam, darling."

He could not have said whether there was mockery in her submissiveness. He spoke to Rabinovitch: "What is Dara's mission?"

"To gather intelligence. You are going to Dhubar under

cover of a diplomat. As your wife, she will use her cover to penetrate the diplomatic community, particularly the Arab missions—they can't resist a woman who shows her face in public, even if they lock their own away."

"I may not be there very long," Durell said.

"If you leave, we will call it an extended temporary assignment. Dara can stay behind until she has established an espionage network. The rest will be routine maintenance."

"It sounds innocent enough," Durell said.

"Of course." There was no innocence in the major's bitter eyes.

"Are you sure that's all?"

"Yes. Except that you will find Dara more than willing to assist you in, ah, removing Princess Ayla."

Dara spoke. "I'll help—any way I can."

"That," Durell said, "is what worries me."

Next, Major Rabinovitch explained that he would be in Dhubar briefly and where he could be found. After that, there was a showing of films taken secretly of Sheik Zeid's party when they were in London for the birth of his son. Then Durell and Dara drove back to the Hertford.

It had been a long day, and Durell was weary.

He almost overlooked the big car parked a few lengths away on Oxford Street—the black and silver Rolls Royce.

Chapter 3

Durell stopped under the high brass awning before the glass door of the hotel, the rain splattering wrinkles of light on the sidewalk and cars sloshing past in the street. He stared back over his shoulder at the Rolls. Its wind-

shield was a pattern of bright rivulets against a black
void. Someone could be inside it. Or in the lobby. Or
waiting in his room.

Before he had time to weigh the matter further, a voice
called: "Mr. Durell?"

He swung his face the other way, saw a dark, out-
sized figure step into the box of light that fell from the
entranceway. A chain of droplets hung from the rim of
his hat, as if he had waited here for some time. His
thick, black mustache glistened in fierce crescents that
almost touched his high cheekbones.

Durell recognized him as Volkan, Prince Tahir's bodyguard.

"What do you want?" Durell asked.

"Princess Nadine has received your message."

"And?"

"She wishes to see you—*simdi,* now." The Turk waved
a hand that looked as if it could palm Durell's head
comfortably.

Durell followed the gesture with his eye and saw the
gleaming Rolls murmur up to the entrance. The driver,
who appeared to be English and probably had been
hired with the car, looked straight ahead. The car's engine
was a whisper above its fat white sidewalls.

Dara looked up at Durell. "This is marvelous, darling.
I get to meet Princess Nadine tonight!"

"I didn't think it would be too soon for you, dear,"
Durell replied in a dry tone. "But first, don't you think
this gentleman should explain why he played tag with us
all over town?"

Dara lowered her eyes. "It would be sweet of him,"
she said.

Durell's eyes went hard against the big Turk's face.
"All right, buster, let's hear it."

"It is so simple, Durell Bey,"—Volkan's cheeks went
taut—"we do not take unexpected guests lightly. Perhaps
you will tell me your business in London."

"Perhaps I won't."

Dara tugged Durell's elbow. "Let's get in the car,
dear."

"Yes, *kafi,* enough." Volkan thrust his fists into the pockets of his raincoat where they stood out like coconuts. "We mustn't keep the princess waiting." He turned with a swift agility that was surprising for his bulk and opened the car door for them.

Inside was a hushed fragrance of leather and expensive woods and carpeting. Volkan rode beside the driver, beyond a glass partition.

"What's she like, Sam, this Princess Nadine?"

"Bright, headstrong, self-centered, beautiful."

"How did you meet her? I thought movie stars were awfully inaccessible."

"Through a friend, Deirdre Padgett." Something small seemed to tumble inside Durell's chest, as always, at the thought of Dee. Their paths crossed seldom enough, but their love had never diminished. "She was writing a fashion story," he continued. "Miss Carroll modeled the clothes. It was in Nice. I happened to be in the neighbor-hood—"

"To see Miss Padgett?"

"My assignment was in the area, so, yes, I was seeing Miss Padgett. She and Nadine became friends. I saw Nadine several times after that. She came to the U.S. occasionally. I never met her family—or that goon up front." Durell nodded at the back of Volkan's thick neck.

Dara slid close to him, knees together, an arm folded through his. She seemed suddenly small in the big car and the presence of the big men. The windshield wipers arced silently to the front of their vision. Traffic had diminished markedly with the late hour.

"Sam?" she said.

"Yes?"

"Maybe it wasn't so smart to crawl into this hearse."

"We won't know for sure until we see what comes of it."

"I don't like the way he followed us, earlier. He may not even be taking us to Princess Nadine's." Her hand made a tentative movement toward the reassurance of the derringer concealed in her bosom.

Gently, Durell pressed her hand back down to her lap.

He blew a short breath through his nose, and said: "It's blindman's buff. You can't win if you don't play."

As the Rolls lumbered deeper into Mayfair, Durell's mind went back to the movies of Sheik Zeid and his party. They had shown Zeid and Princess Ayla and Ayla's parents, Nadine and Tahir. Two Turkish bodyguards had been in evidence, Volkan and a man named Yilmaz, who stayed close to Princess Ayla. But for the bodyguards, the group might have been any wealthy family on a holiday. All wore Western clothing. Sheik Zeid, a short, solid figure with a toothbrush mustache also wore a Bedouin *ghutra* headcloth with his tailored suit. An enterprising Shin Beth agent had obtained a sequence of Princess Ayla at Regent's Park, in blue jeans, shortly after her release from the hospital. Durell supposed the jeans were a holdover from her undergraduate days at Hunter College, where she had majored in political science. She was startlingly beautiful, endowed with her movie-star mother's figure and her father's dark almond eyes. Her black hair glistened like a sequined cape.

Princess Ayla hadn't seemed very happy in those films, Durell reflected. She had looked tense and tired and had done little to return the small gestures of affection displayed by Sheik Zeid—the little courtesy, a touch of a hand, a slow smile.

There had been no doubt, however, of the fondness she had shown for her mother, who had lost none of the good looks once referred to as "platinum lightning." Nadine was smaller than her daughter and perfectly proportioned, with pearly skin, round blue eyes, and a stubborn chin.

The tall frame of Prince Tahir had loomed over the group. He carried himself with the bearing of a born aristocrat and seemed to favor ascots and crushable wool fedoras. His chiseled face was dark and brooding beneath charcoal brows, and his lips bore a twist that was imperial and pernicious.

The Rolls parked in front of a large brick and stone dwelling of Victorian vintage. Murky light came as if from a distant room through draperies that were drawn not quite closed. Water trickled down the gutter, splattered in weighty drops from leaf to leaf in a stubby, much-pruned quince tree as they waited behind the big Turk while he opened the door.

They entered single file, Volkan stepping aside for Dara first, then Durell. The Turk felt as big as the Tower of London behind Durell's back as they walked through a carpeted entryway into a dimly lighted hallway and stopped before high double doors with ornate brass and crystal knobs. Volkan, saying nothing, reached past them and twisted a knob, pushed a door, nodded them inside.

At first all Durell saw in the low light was a large parlor, immaculately kept and last furnished about the turn of the century. There were dark velvet draperies, massive footstools with gargoyles' legs, potted palms, and even a gilded cupid that bore a frosted fishbowl lighting fixture on its head. On the left an organ cabineted in wood dark as the rainy night occupied a space slightly smaller than a London bus.

Then Nadine stepped into view, breathtaking in a dress of black panne velvet that was long and tight, outlining the curve of hip and thigh, and open-toed silver slippers.

The chromed and elaborately engraved .25 automatic she held could have been spun from her platinum hair.

"Now," she said, "I'm going to rid myself of a spy."

Chapter 4

A pinched gasp caught in Dara's throat.

Durell took no time to think about it.

He knocked her roughly aside and leaped for Nadine,

aware of Volkan's hulk behind him. Nadine went sprawling, silver heels kicking the air, and he was on top of her,
the gun enfolded in his hand, his thumb behind the trigger.
Skin prickled at the back of his neck as he expected
Volkan to pounce. He could only hope that Dara would
cover for him. Nadine's breath came into his face in
angry squirts as they grappled, and he smelled her hot
toilet fragrances, his nose close to the smooth stem of her
neck.

It only lasted a second.

"Sam—? *Sam!*" Nadine's voice was exasperated.

He froze at the odd tone of her words, looked into her
face, saw half-moons of white that curved around
enormous blue irises.

Then the room exploded with Volkan's laughter.
Durell twisted a bewildered face up at the mountainous
Turk. "She meant me, Durell Bey." Volkan bellowed
with glee, held his sides as he shook and heaved.

Dara stood stiffly next to the dark wainscotting of the
wall, a hand over her breast as if in fright—but Durell
knew the derringer was beneath that hand and that
Volkan was luckier than he could have imagined.

"She meant that I am a spy, Durell Bey," Volkan
gasped. He rubbed the moist slits of his eyes. "She
doesn't like me very much," he said.

Nadine scrambled to her feet, smoothed her dress.
Springs of hair had been wrenched from her immaculately
piled coiffure and stood out at the back of her neck.
Her face was flushed and angry. She had surrendered
the .25, a baby Heckler & Koch, to Durell.

"I knew you'd come, Sam," she snapped, "but I didn't
think it would be like this."

"Me neither." Durell studied Volkan, then looked back
at her.

"I mean her no harm." Volkan's laughing fit had
passed. He spoke soberly now. "Prince Tahir has left me
to watch over her. She is a difficult woman."

Nadine shouted. "He's spying on me, I tell you!" She
twisted, and her eyes darted about the room. She looked
as if she wanted something to throw.

"Relax, Nadine," Durell said. "Get hold of yourself."

"*Evet*—yes—relax," Volkan seconded. He had his hat off now. The low light glowed greasily on his shaven head.

"You get out," Durell said.

"Me?" Volkan drew himself up until his shadow seemed to cover half the wall, and his eyes narrowed to dark slits. "Princess Nadine is my responsibility. I have orders—"

Durell made the little .25 evident in his hand and spoke in a low voice. "Get the hell out."

Volkan's eyes clouded with uncertainty, but before he could respond, Nadine cried: "No, Sam—don't let him go. He's up to something. I don't trust him. I don't trust any of them."

Durell had no way of knowing how much of this was hysterics, dramatics, how much the truth. Certainly Nadine was frightened. She had fought her way up from an Alabama sharecropper's shack to the palaces of the glittering Mediterranean world. He had known she was tough. He had never seen her scared, but she was now. And she reacted like a trapped alley cat.

He tried to calm her. "Listen. He's leaving now. He won't harm you."

Volkan's tone was serious. "I would not," he said. "I am only obeying—"

"All right! Get out!" Nadine screamed. "Get out, you—you oaf!"

An ash tray flashed through the air, and Volkan flinched as it crashed against the wall an inch from his ear. She got her hands around another missile, a vase this time, but Volkan dodged through the door a fraction before it splintered behind him.

The momentary silence rang in Durell's ears.

Then Nadine breathed deeply and spoke in a tired voice. "You shouldn't have let him go. We could have taken him. Well, at least you're here, thank God. Got a cigarette?"

"Sorry."

She went about the room, opened and slammed cabinet doors. "Damn Tahir! He took them all, every last one."

Suddenly she held Durell's lapels. "He's always trying to run my life. Damn Turk! Help me, Sam. They've worn me down." She sighed against his chest. She did not look worn down. She looked twenty years younger than her age, Durell thought.

Abruptly: "Who's that girl?"

Durell's gaze followed Nadine's slender arm and saw it was pointed at Dara, who stood and looked not quite amused in the shadows near the door through which Volkan had darted.

"She's my wife," Durell said.

Nadine's face turned up, her cheek against his chest. "Why?"

"What do you mean?"

"You always loved Deirdre."

"It's none of your business, Nadine."

Nadine's big blue eyes stared cruelly at Dara for a moment.

"How do you do, Princess Nadine," Dara ventured.

"Can the princess bit, honey." She took a sad breath and shook her lovely head. "Sam, it's unreal to have honest-to-God people around me for a change."

Tears came into her eyes, and Durell wondered if they were authentic or the product of a mind that sometimes manufactured what it wished to bolster its fantasies. He patted her back gently. "Sit down," he said.

"Hell, I'm not an invalid." She pushed away.

"Look, if you don't like Volkan, why don't you fire him?"

She made a sound of pretended amusement. "I can't. He's Tahir's man." An edge of anger returned to her voice. "He spies on me, Sam. They're plotting to kill me. I don't fit in, so they're going to slit my throat and stuff me in a sewer."

"Fit in with what?" Dara questioned. She moved toward Nadine, leaving the door for the first time.

Nadine's bosom lifted in a dramatic sigh, and she rolled her eyes. "Oh, I wish I knew. Sit down, honey." She waved a limp hand toward a garish Victorian sofa.

"It's Tahir's doing; darling little Ayla finally got her prince, now Tahir's strutting around like a king."

"Is he in the house?" Durell asked. Dara sat on the edge of the sofa, primly erect.

"He's gone. They're all gone. I'm all that's left. Me and the gorilla." She made a long face and sighed again. "You see, there's no place in Tahir's future for me. We don't even live together anymore. He's jealous of my influence with Ayla, though. That's why he doesn't divorce me. I could call it quits, I suppose, and go live in the States. But who would call me princess then? And it's too late to go back to the movies." She smiled wistfully.

"Go to Istanbul. You have a house there," Durell said.

"Yes!" Nadine listened intently.

"But first contact Princess Ayla for me. Tell her to expect me—I'll be in Dhubar tomorrow."

"Shh!" Nadine pressed a finger to his lips. "Don't mention that too loudly." She rolled her big blue eyes toward the door. "Volkan will be listening," she whispered.

Durell lowered his voice. "You'll call her?"

"Sure. She didn't want to go there in the first place. Tahir made her do it."

"Forced her?"

"Bullied her."

"What about Sheik Zeid?"

Nadine showed her small palms. "He thinks she wanted to go—he offered to allow her to stay here for the time being."

"It doesn't look too bad, then," Durell mused. "I'll get her out safely and quietly."

"Can you do that? I know you're with the government. . . ."

"There are ways. Once out, she must contact Sheik Zeid and explain that she left of her own free will. Of course, she could leave on her own, if she'd just tell him how she feels."

"But she won't! That's the trouble. She's scared to death of her father, and he's there. This is the only way." She fell back on the overstuffed couch as if exhausted. "I just thank my lucky stars for you, Sam."

"Then you'll return to Istanbul?"

"Why not? I'll be glad to get out of this museum—just look at it! It just suited Tahir, it's just like a Turk."

"Then we'll be going," Durell said.

"Oh, no. You spend the night here."

Durell looked at her.

"I had Volkan check you out and bring your bags with you."

"What?"

"All I have is you—and your lovely little wife, of course." A thin shadow appeared between Nadine's perfectly plucked brows. "She's awfully young, Sam." She turned back to him. "You *will* spend the night. Don't let that big old bear Volkan get me. Say you will!"

Dara stared at Durell. He sighed and nodded to Nadine.

"Did you always love this girl named Deirdre?" There was a long silence as Dara stood uncertainly in the bathroom doorway.

"Yes," Durell replied. He saw her shadow in a carpet of light that fell from the bathroom door. He looked back at her, from where he lay on the bed. The light behind her cast a fringe of fire around her straw-blond hair. She wore a modest robe of peach-colored tricot. He saw a scallop of lace beneath its hem.

"I'll sleep in the chair," she said, and came barefoot into the room, hugging the robe closed. It whispered around her thighs.

"Not if you're my wife." Durell threw back the covers on the other side of the bed.

"You're carrying this a bit far."

"It wasn't my idea. You don't know who might come through that door. We have to be convincing." Durell felt the presence of Volkan, perhaps at the other end of the house, maybe just outside the door. It was possible that Nadine had been indulging herself with her theatrical display of fright and rage. So far, Volkan had kept himself above reproach except for tailing them earlier. And even that was understandable as an excess of virtue, if his job included screening Nadine's callers. Durell did not know what to think.

The bathroom went dark, and the walls swam with muzzy, distracting afterimages; then the soft gray of the city's nightglow settled over everything. The rain had picked up, and the shower drummed against French doors to a terrace. The lights of London came through black tree-shapes out there. Durell felt the bed sink with Dara's weight and heard her low voice: "This is strictly business, Sam."

"Are you still wearing the derringer around your neck?"

"Yes."

"Then what are you worried about?"

He heard a rustle of bedcovers, and the sweet aroma of bathpowder touched his nose.

Dara spoke through the darkness. "Do you really think you can get Princess Ayla to leave Dhubar?"

"We'll have to wait and see."

"Sheik Zeid loves her very much, they say. If she runs out on him, he may never allow her to return—she must understand the risk. He could be vengeful. You know an Arab's pride."

"While we're on the darker side of things—it would be embarrassing if he found out we were providing cover for you."

"We don't wish to harm him, Sam. Heaven knows we can use all the moderates we can get among the Arabs, and we want him to retain his throne—whatever happens to the Thirteenth Princess. If he loses it, all of Dhubar's wealth could go to promote another round of war in the Middle East, more terrible than ever. My mission is only to gather information."

"Try to tell him that," Durell said in a dry tone.

He felt a toss of Dara's slender frame. She blew a breath. "If only it weren't for Princess Ayla. . . ."

"We have to play the cards we've been dealt," Durell said. "This is a hand where nobody folds."

It seemed a long while before Dara's breathing took the deep, slow rhythm of slumber. Durell remained awake.

The ancient city rumbled and glowed. The hoot of a freighter came from the Thames.

He relaxed slowly and reluctantly, the presence of Volkan an unknown quantity on his mind. When he entered a twilight state of rest, the nightmare in the hotel room came back to him, and he drowsily shook it from his mind.

He did not sleep in the ordinary sense.

Something high in his brain never quite stopped weighing and testing, perceiving his surroundings.

The sound of gunfire started at the back of Dara's mind, as from a well, in ebony blackness, and she knew the dream was coming again.

The spitting, mechanical hammering became a clutter of violent noises, explosions, screams, the rattle of falling debris on the hard earth a few miles from the Sea of Galilee.

Fourteen-year-old Dara peered with frightened eyes from the window of her cinder-block house. Men in *ghutras* and crazy striped clothing, pants tucked into boots, ran out of the black thicket that was an orange grove and into the moonlight, rifles winking. They ran like monkeys, bent over, and brought the rattle of death up the row of little houses. Something snicked at the window frame, and Dara heard glass shatter near her ear. At the same moment one of the dark figures hurled something into the window of another house and ran on, and the house came apart with tongues of flame shooting out the cracks.

Now men darted out of the little houses, half-clothed, carrying rifles that jerked and snapped, and many of them seemed to stumble over something and fall on their faces and just lie there. The bonfire of an automobile cast a yellow glow over everything as the crazy-striped intruders scrurried on up the slope toward Dara's house.

They were very close now, and Dara's eyes seemed to fill her freckled face with great, milky pools of fear in the moonlight, but she did not leave the window, didn't even think to.

"Dara! Get down!" It was her mother.

She heard her mother's frantic breath and the slap of her bare feet as she ran across the floor toward the window. Behind her was the wail of her brother, scarcely noticeable in the confused racket.

"I said get down, girl! Under the bed!" Dara had never seen such a look on her mother's face. Her mother yanked her arm and slapped her face, and she could see tears on her mother's cheeks and the anguished gleam of teeth clenched in her mouth.

Dara was bawling, disoriented in the dark bedlam as she scrambled on all fours.

The room flashed white and orange. The brilliant stroke of light sucked all the breath out of her.

There was no sound.

There was nothing.

It was gray dawn when feeling returned, and Dara found herself clawing for air from under tumbled debris. A hand discovered her. Shattered boards and stone were lifted away, and she was hauled gently into the cool, smoke-smudged air.

And this was the worst part of the dream:

A sad-faced woman showed her to the sheet-covered bodies of her mother and little brother. She fell to her knees and clawed at her cheeks. Her lips and face and eyes screamed, "Mother! Brother!"—but no sound came out.

If only she could bring forth the agony that tore her insides.

Now she had no family—her father had died in the molten cradle of a tank in the Sinai in June, 1967.

And now all she could see in the dream was her face, screaming silently for all that was lost.

Sometime during the night a small, sharp noise awakened Durell from his twilight sleep, and he sat up, his .38 in his grip, the odor of its gun oil heavy in his nostrils.

Then Dara whimpered again and cried out.

A thin alarm of half-opened eyes shone in her face as she stared up at him, her breath ragged and light.

"It was only a nightmare," he said.

She nodded. Her short hair was spread like a crown on the pillow. She made no move for the reassurance of his arms.

"It's all over," he said as he tucked his gun back under the sheets.

"It will never be all over," she replied.

"Want to talk about it?"

"No."

A pale banana light of morning filled the room when Durell awakened again. Dara's cheek was against her pillow, her breath soft through a curtain of polished teeth. He sensed that something was not quite right, moved his eyes about the room, gun under his palm, tendons tensing. It had stopped raining. Durell felt the city stirring out there beyond the wall of the gloomy terrace. Something had disturbed him, but he did not know what.

Then his eyes fixed on a darker shadow behind an overgrown alder bush, but quite near the French doors.

It was Volkan.

Lazily, Durell rolled onto his side and planted his lips over Dara's warm, pliant mouth. Her eyelids sprung open, and he felt her hands push adamantly against his shoulders. Her robe did nothing to dampen the erotic pressure of her breasts as she struggled for an astonished breath. Then she saw Durell signal toward the terrace with his eyes, and whispered: "What's he doing?"

"Checking up on the deck," Durell muttered.

"Well—we mustn't look like a fifth ace." She smiled, and her arms pulled him harder against her. Abruptly her kiss developed sincerity.

Durell glanced toward the terrace again—Volkan was gone, apparently satisfied that Durell and Dara were the honeymooners they had said they were. Reluctantly, he started to pull away from the scented softness of Dara's body, but she held him with surprising strength. Her hazel eyes were fevered, her face a pink blush against the white pillow case.

"We should get dressed and pack," he said.

"In a little while."

"It's only an hour and a half until our plane leaves."

She kissed him and nuzzled his neck, and the roundings of her body pressed against him, as she said:

"I want to fly *now*."

Chapter 5

TURKISH BITCH
  OTTOMAN WHORE
  DOWN WITH THE THIRTEENTH PRINCESS

A score of such signs and banners, in sweeping Arabic letters, fluttered and rattled in the hot breeze at Dhubar Airport. They hung from a high chain link fence near the new terminal building, behind which a mob had awaited the arrival of Princess Ayla two nights before. She and Sheik Zeid had been escorted from the airport to the city by a column of heavily armed troops.

That the signs remained was indication enough of a government still off-balance and fighting for its life, Durell thought as he stood on the scorching gravel of the airport parking lot and argued with Patrick McNamara.

"Send her back, Sam. It's really unsafe."

"Dara stays," Durell told the pink-faced man.

"I never thought I'd see you act like a lovestruck dope," McNamara said, and his pale blue eyes changed from nervous to annoyed. He was slope-shouldered, powerfully built, and had a seamed, sunburned face that could change its character second by second. Normally, it held a warning of secrecy, the threat of forbidden knowledge, but Durell knew that you could never be really sure what he was thinking.

"There won't be any other women," McNamara said. "Just the locals. The embassies have sent all their dependents out."

"I'm willing to take my chances with my husband," Dara said.

"Aw—!" McNamara cursed beneath his breath. "Get in the car then."

"Never mind," Durell said. "The embassy was to have had a car waiting for us." His head felt as if the sun had it in a vise, out here in the open. The lemon sky hurt his eyes with its fierce brilliance, and shimmering mirages to the east made a plate that held the haze-gray rumple of Dhubar City. The temperature must have been 120°. "We'll wait for the embassy car," Durell said.

"There won't be an embassy car; I'm taking you under my wing," McNamara said.

"I don't want your wing. I'm regular embassy personnel."

McNamara's deeply grooved face changed from considerate to skeptical. "Sure, Sam. Like butterflies have balls—excuse me, little lady. Don't try to kid an old kidder, Sam."

Durell said nothing. McNamara's hand wiped sweat from the hairy V of his open-necked, short-sleeved shirt. They stared at each other.

Dara broke the silence. "Oh, let's ride with Mr. McNamara. What difference does it make, Sam, darling?"

"Listen to the little lady, Sam. You know I could get you both sent straight back to where you came from—"

"Not if you value your cozy ties with Washington," Durell said.

"Don't throw that up to me," McNamara said in a brusque tone. Then, more thoughtfully: "You know, the time has come when I can do without you easier than you can do without Dhubar. I don't know why you're here, but you remember this: Dhubar is my turf. I'm going to keep an eye on you." He grinned—but it wasn't a grin.

Durell put Dara into the car and got in beside her.

Baking sand and stone lay in every direction as they drove toward the city. The webbed spires of oil drilling rigs were everywhere, and the pure desert air was fouled with the stench of natural gas. The sudden splurge of mineral wealth had put the old of Dhubar on a collision course with the westernized Twentieth Century, Durell thought, as they passed a shepherd boy tending scrawny goats near a Bedouin tent with a new pickup truck parked beside it.

Durell had not cared for the omens in McNamara's pink, vulpine face—and he had been taught to read faces by an expert, his Grandpa Jonathan, one of the last Mississippi River gamblers. The home of Durell's boyhood had been on board Jonathan's beached side-wheeler, *Trois Belles,* and every stroll through its ornate salon, with its roulette wheel and card tables, had brought to his grandfather's mind another story to tell, another lesson to be learned. There, amid the moss-hung oaks of Bayou Pêche Rouge, under the hot Louisiana sun, Durell had learned when to raise and when to fold—and to judge the will and cunning of his opponents.

The minarets of Dhubar, seen through the dancing heat, came closer as Durell considered Patrick Kelly McNamara, who ran what was arguably the largest, most professional and best-funded intelligence operation in the Middle East, barring only Israel's. The archconservative old emir had despised all creeds, political or otherwise, that did not spring from the tenets of Islam. He suppressed the communists and socialists and republicans with relatively little cruelty and no consistency, but he was fanatical and undeviating in his demand to know who they were and what they were doing at all times. When tremendous oil wealth had come his way, he used it to carry his fanatical quest beyond the borders of tiny Dhubar, with its population of scarcely one million, and eventually came to know what political plagues and irreligious epidemics sprouted throughout the Arab world.

This huge budget and store of information had made McNamara a powerful man in his own right.

A document from him could seal the doom of a man two thousand miles away.

Money had been no object when the old emir asked the CIA to build him the most modern intelligence apparatus from the ground up, and McNamara had been tapped to honcho the project in its pilot stage. He'd had more experience than anyone in the Mideast, had served as Central in Cairo, Riyadh, Damascus, Ankara, and Athens. McNamara had taken the job and resigned from K Section in his prime. Then the old emir had asked him to stay on permanently.

K Section could afford to be philosophical about its loss. McNamara still maintained close ties with Washington that were ultrasecret. It was one of those arrangements that thrive on mutual self-interest.

But McNamara was a man of divided loyalties.

Durell did not trust him.

He remembered the man who had ambushed him in London and looked back, through the rear window, as they drove through a large section of new, concrete workers' houses. Each had a small, walled courtyard and a window air conditioner. The old emir had done something to share the country's wealth with its people, but there was a long way to go.

Durell did not see anyone behind them.

McNamara's Cadillac entered a broad, palm-lined boulevard flanked with parks where whirling sprinklers spewed water in fiery, prismatic streams. Dirty smoke rose from the town's old quarter and was torn by the Persian Gulf wind. Beyond the city, with its ribs of shadowed alleys, its mud houses and sparkling high rises, he saw great columns of dense, black smoke given off by flaming pools of slush crude oil.

Fire should have been the national emblem of Dhubar, he thought, instead of a golden scimitar on a blue background. Everything burned to the touch, and the wind that stirred sand in the gutters hit you like a blowtorch.

They passed a low, crenelated tower, all that remained of the city's ancient mud-brick wall. Another sprinkler-irrigated park surrounded it, recalling the Arabs' love of water and shady places.

A large gathering hove into view, and McNamara wove the car carefully through a surly crowd where soldiers savagely beat eight prisoners who were chained to parking meters. Two of the prisoners had slumped to the street, dead or unconscious. The crowd watched in stony silence, their eyes filled with hatred for the soldiers, who worked methodically, their khaki shirts soaking with sweat. The onlookers filled the street and were stubborn about parting to make way for the big black car with the tinted windows.

Durell exchanged tense glances with Dara.

Nothing happened.

Soldiers lounged in the shade of awnings and held their M-16s casually. Here and there were a smashed window, a fire-scorched building, a looted shop. The Dhubar Oil Company headquarters had been gutted. Junk littered the sidewalks, bottles, paper, scraps of cloth; and imprecations against the Thirteenth Princess were scrawled on walls. Most shops were shuttered on the boulevard, and there was little traffic, although Durell noted a fair amount of activity on the side streets. The big avenues seemed to be no-man's-lands, set aside for violence.

McNamara twisted the wheel, and the car veered onto a street that ran along the bay front. A trooper with a holstered .45 waved them around a Shorland armored car of British manufacture, and Durell remembered that Dhubar had been a British protectorate until the last decade.

"Most of the fires are out," McNamara said. It was the first time he had spoken since leaving the airport.

"There will be more tonight, to judge by that crowd we passed," Durell said.

"It won't be so easy for them this time."

"Don't expect the curfew to stop them. How is morale in the army?"

"As good as can be expected. They don't like shooting their own people, of course."

A pink scatter of flamingoes rose from the turquoise bay, up-shore from the stone breakwater of the old harbor.

The new port, in the middle distance, was packed with hundreds of new automobiles, dumped to bake in the sun until means for distributing them could be found. Freighters bearing every kind of goods from the industrial world stood far out into the gulf, waiting their turn at the overloaded docks. Beyond the new port and the recently completed desalinization plant, was the two-mile-long bulk-oil loading pier, with its own flock of tankers and supertankers.

Up beside them the Arabian fishing boats and coasters were reduced to toys. The old harbor, nearby, was port for most of the dhows, and there were various types, *sambuks, booms, haggalas, zarooks,* each hull a bit different. Several were hauled up on the beach for bottom scraping and painting with camel fat and lime, but no one was working on them.

The city was not deserted, but it felt deserted, Durell thought. It had a neglected, despairing air. It didn't help that the walls of the older buildings were the bleak reds and browns of dried mud.

A man with a donkey loaded with camel's-thorn firewood ambled along.

A woman covered totally in a black *burka* darted into an alley with a basket of fish.

Bullets hit the roof of the car with a sound like a steel chain.

Chapter 6

A hot breath blew past Durell's neck, and he winced as a lead splinter sliced his cheek.

The car slewed around, the buildings and soldiers out

there whirling crazily past the tinted windows, and Durell saw that Dara was on the floor. He did not have time to wonder if she had been hit, for as the car rocked to a halt, the savage sound of a chain slap came again, and webs of shattered glass fringed bullet holes beside his face.

"Get this car moving again, God damn it!" he yelled to McNamara. Soldiers ducked and loped for cover.

"Shit! For crissakes . . . !" McNamara twisted the ignition key, but nothing happened.

Dara stirred, looked up with a face so white that her small freckles stood out like inkspots. For the first time scent came into the air conditioned car, and Durell smelled curry and the filth of open latrines. Then he heard a clatter of automatic rifle fire and saw flowers of dust high up on the side of an office building, where the soldiers aimed. They raised up from behind a parked truck and squeezed out their magazines and hunched down, pressing their backs against the side of the truck.

The sky was blinding, behind the office building.

Everything made harsh shadows.

It was like being on a checkerboard.

"Can't you start the car?" Durell's apprehension gave way to an impatient anger. Dara clawed for a door-handle, the useless little derringer in her hand. Durell pushed her back to the floor, gave a guttural curse, grabbed McNamara's shirt collar, and yanked him aside. He hurled himself over the seat, sweat pouring down his face.

A third stuttering crash stippled the trunk lid, and ricochets wailed and sighed into the distance.

It was as if the gunman had targeted on the rear of the car. Durell felt a shiver of rage and dismay: this was the same kind of greeting he'd received in London—a welcome of death.

The soldiers fired up at the building. Everything was confusion. Then Durell realized the gearshift was still in drive, swore, slammed it into park, hit the ignition.

Troops ran back and forth across the street. A 12.7 mm. machine gun opened up from the back of a scout car parked in a side street, and the tall building puffed concrete dust, showered sparkling, twisting shards of glass into the wind.

The car started.

Durell jammed the accelerator to the floor, glanced at McNamara, saw his cheeks quiver with rage. They rocketed down the street, the car wobbling crazily on a ruptured tire, and Durell chose the first side street, slammed on the brakes, fishtailed the car through an arch into a busy *souk*. The Cadillac took down a striped awning and sent bushels of dates, rice, and limes scattering through the marketplace. A shopkeeper in a *tarbush* cap shrieked and wailed, and a crowd gathered—as Durell had suspected, the narrow, fetid byways of the city buzzed with life.

Dara popped out of the car first, looked back and forth, lips parted, heart pumping visibly in the veins of her neck. Durell calmed the shopkeeper with a wad of dinars. His hand shook slightly as he wiped blood from the thin gash on his cheek. McNamara just leaned against the car for a moment and lighted a cigarette. The crowd cackled and pointed at the bullet holes as they milled about the damaged car. The crackle of gunfire still came from the street, around the corner. Here, though, donkeys brayed and camels growled—there was even an aroma of mutton, hot on charcoal braziers, and the lilt and clash of a *takht* ensemble.

"Where do you get off, yanking me around like that?" McNamara demanded, when he'd got his breath.

"You acted like a damned fool, slamming on the brakes," Durell shot back.

"I thought I'd run over something. I heard the impact." McNamara's red face showed no apology. "Don't ever put your hands on me again," he said.

"Just be thankful you're still alive," Durell said.

"Don't say I didn't warn you—how's your chick?" Durell's eyes went to Dara. She looked incredibly cool and unruffled now, against the two tense, combative men. Her derringer had disappeared back into the scarf-shrouded recess between her breasts.

"I came out of it as well as you." Her tone was impertinent. "It is strange that only the back half of the car was damaged."

"It certainly is," Durell said and looked bluntly at McNamara.

The other's face was offended. "Jesus, some creep can't shoot straight, and now you're going to blame me for setting you up."

"Did you?" Durell asked.

McNamara threw his cigarette to the cobbles. "What am I supposed to say? Yes?" His face was open, but there was a wall behind his eyes.

Life was returning to a semblance of normality around the *souk,* with its fly-covered sheep carcasses and cubbyhole artisan shops, when a Jeep roared into the street and slowed with whining transmission behind the Cadillac. It was equipped with a recoilless rifle and ranging machine gun. It backed and filled, squashing spilled dates and scattering bystanders, and came to rest in a triangle of shade at the entrance to the larger street where the shooting had taken place. A shell was thrust home, the ranging gun sputtered, and a blast of yellow flame shot backward, setting fire to the fallen awning.

The shopkeeper started shrieking again and ran in circles of dismay.

Durell heard the crash of the shell into the office building.

McNamara said, "Let's get out of here."

"What about that triggerman?" Durell asked.

"The army will take care of that bastard."

"He should be questioned."

"You want to walk through the cross fire to do it?" McNamara spit into the filthy street. His eyes were quizzical. "What the hell are you doing here, Cajun?"

"Maybe I came to help you."

"Ha, ha."

"We value your cooperation. We don't want to lose you."

Suspicion swarmed thick as the marketplace flies in McNamara's eyes. "So—?"

"So I'll help you put your act together. You're vulnerable. For once you know too many people in too many places. How does Sheik Zeid know that you didn't set up the assassination, for whatever reason?" McNamara listened, his face blunt and strained. Encouraged, Durell continued: "There's certain to be a nasty purge, once Sheik Zeid gets his footing—the assassination of his father will be paid for in rolling heads. When judgment comes, you can be all alone, or you can have the most powerful country in the world in your corner, ready to say a few good words—provided you convince me you weren't in on the plot."

"You son of a bitch," McNamara growled. "You work fast, don't you? You've only been here half an hour, and you've already made your move to neutralize me. You want to get me so busy covering my own ass that I won't have time to wonder what you're doing here."

McNamara's canny perception jarred Durell, but he did not let it show. The man was as clever as his reputation said. Durell just stared at him for a second and saw a shadow of uncertainty cross the other's eyes. The only thing to do, Durell decided, was to raise his own bluff. He turned to Dara, and said: "Come on, dear. Let's find a taxi and go back to the airport. I'll just have to tell General McFee that Pat chose to go down with his ship."

He felt McNamara's grip on his arm. "Now wait a minute, Sam,"—the man sucked a short, defeated breath— "what do you suggest?"

"I'd like to ask the assassin some questions."

"He's dead." McNamara was irritable. "They beat him to death during the interrogation."

Durell looked up at the sky, as if considering this. Sweat had soaked his shirt, beneath the lightweight jacket of his gray suit, and his collar hung open, the tie loosened for a breath of air. "Can you get me a transcript of the interrogation?" he asked.

"I don't see what good it will do, but I guess there's no harm. I'll meet you at your hotel in half an hour," McNamara said.

FILE: Z 239–1

COPY: 1 of 1 (English translation)

CLASS: SECRET SECRET SECRET

ROUTE: Col. Patrick K. McNamara, RIB

SUBJECT: Interrogation transcript of Prisoner Ali Ben Rashid. Present were Dr. Ahmed Nassir, interrogator, and two assistants. Also Col. Zaki Aziz, chief of security police; Col. Patrick K. McNamara, Royal Intelligence Bureau.

FIRST SESSION: 1225 hrs.

PRISONER: Requests medical attention.

NASSIR: You will speak when spoken to. State your full name, nationality, place of residence.

PRISONER: I told that to the police, sir.

NASSIR: Now, will you obey my order?

PRISONER: Ali Ben Rashid; Dhubaran; No. 10 Buraidah Street, Dhubar.

NASSIR: That is a lie. No one there has ever heard of you.

PRISONER: It is true . . . (indistinguishable).

NASSIR: Now will you tell the truth?

PRISONER: Requests medical attention.

NASSIR: Why did you kill His Royal Highness?

PRISONER: For my Arab brothers.

NASSIR: Who are your Arab brothers? Consider your answer well.

PRISONER: All Arabs.

NASSIR: Revive the prisoner. (The prisoner is revived.) What were you saying?

PRISONER: What?

NASSIR: You spoke in a foreign tongue just now. A dog's language. What was it? What were you saying?

PRISONER: I speak only Arabic.

NASSIR: Now, what tongue?

PRISONER: What is the question, sir? May I have—

NASSIR: Wake up the jackal. (The prisoner is revived.) We know you came from Cyprus this afternoon. You flew on Dhubar Royal Airlines.

PRISONER: I have friends in Nicosia.

NASSIR: Who? What friends?

PRISONER: They—they are not involved in this. I am alone in this.

NASSIR: You lie again. I warn you, we will get it out of you, sooner or later. Who paid you to shoot His Highness?"

PRISONER: No one, sir.

NASSIR: Who put you up to it?

PRISONER: No one.

NASSIR: Revive the prisoner.
(The prisoner does not respond. Interrogation suspended.)

SECOND SESSION: 1322 hrs.

NASSIR: You have had time to reconsider?

PRISONER: Yes, sir. May I see a doctor?

NASSIR: Later, perhaps. Have a cigarette. Tell us now, who sent you to assassinate His Highness?

PRISONER: No one, sir.

NASSIR: You have a wife? A girl friend, perhaps? We will find out. I'm warning you, it will be easier on her if you cooperate.

PRISONER: I am cooperating.

NASSIR: Revive the prisoner. . . .

It went on for twenty-three more pages, as Durell sat reading in the red-and-gold-decorated cubicle of his modern hotel room. The management had stuck giants Xs of masking tape across the plate-glass balcony windows. Beyond the Xs was a view of an emerald swimming pool where no one swam and of dockside activity that extended into the dim distance, where supertankers took on their cargo. Closer was the royal palace, with a clock in its minaretlike tower and the bay water lapping at its walls.

Durell turned back to the transcript, the stench of the scorched lobby tainting the air even up here, four floors above the street.

The final session had begun at 1430 hours and lasted only fifteen minutes. It was clear that Col. Dr. Nassir hadn't had much to work with by then.

It began with the prisoner pleading for a drink of water, begging for medical attention.

It ended with:

PRISONER: No response.

(A medical doctor having been summoned, PRISONER was pronounced dead at 1446 hrs.)

Durell tossed the sheaf of legal-sized typescript onto the bed. He heard Dara showering, trying to shake off the heat.

"I told you there wasn't anything there," McNamara said. He sipped his gin and tonic and watched Durell.

"What about that Nicosia bit?"

"We've checked it as best we could. It's a blank wall."

Durell stood and stretched the muscles of his long legs. The hot wind brushed date palms on the street below and stirred eddies of sand in a corner of the balcony. A Caltex tanker, its black funnel bearing a red star, moved up the slot of the Dhubar channel. In the momentary silence, McNamara took a cigarette from the pocket of his expensive print shirt.

Durell spoke first. "Why did you let them kill him?"

"Hell, I couldn't stop it. These people have their ways."

His blue eyes looked suddenly amused. "They weren't so happy about it themselves. They hung him anyhow, strung him up in the sheep market, already dead. He's still there, for all I know."

"You could have stopped it, if you'd tried," Durell persisted. He tightened the screws a bit. "If Sheik Zeid begins' to wonder why the best source of information he had was murdered. . . ." He did not trouble to finish the sentence.

"Ah, shit. It's over and done with, Cajun. Maybe I didn't handle it the best way at the time, but put yourself in my place. It was chaos, man. Everybody pissing all over themselves."

"Tell that to Sheik Zeid." Durell stared at him.

McNamara's gaze turned inward, and suddenly he did not look too well. He seemed to have forgotten the cigarette that dangled loosely in his fingers. Durell almost felt compassion for the man, then put the emotion out of his mind, annoyed at its intrusion. He had to control McNamara until he had completed his mission. He had to control him however he could, and that meant a dangerous game.

Durell spoke again. "You had a personal relationship with the old emir, Pat. But Sheik Zeid is going to measure you from a distance. Show your loyalty by taking the initiative. Go to the high command; get their approval to close your borders and maintain air surveillance over them—if arms are being smuggled in, you've got to stop it. Otherwise you'll have a second Beirut here."

McNamara sat up. "Close our borders? That would be a slap in the face for our neighbors, an accusation."

"Since when did you worry about being diplomatic?"

"Since Sheik Zeid became emir."

Dara came out of the bathroom looking lovely, tiny strands of blond hair sticking to the back of her neck, above a severely tailored black dress she intended to wear to the emir's reception. She ignored the men as she made minor adjustments to its neckline.

"All right," Durell told McNamara, dropping the transcript into the other's lap, "but this is the lousiest interrogation I've ever seen. Your Dr. Nassir was nothing more than a sadistic killer. Given competent methods, you'd have had it all in a week."

"Yeah? Who's got a week?" McNamara rolled the transcript in his hand and paused at the door. "Stay out of trouble," he said, and then he went out.

Durell did not know what the man might do next.

He did not care, so long as McNamara left him breathing room.

"You played him like a fish, Sam," Dara said, and sat on the bed. "Why so gloomy?"

"It was almost too easy—why do I feel like there's a hook in my jaw?"

She lifted a brow and her sharply defined lips smiled. "Maybe that hook is on the end of *my* line."

Durell's dark blue eyes did not return the smile. He telephoned for a rental car to take them to the reception. The sun went below the horizon in an enormous explosion of gold and salmon hues, and the cloudless sky turned oyster gray. Beyond the city the desert was an endless, murky purple, starred by the orange twinkle of oil-field flares and the vertical strings of drilling rig lights.

As they waited for the car, Dara said: "You don't let people comfort you when you're troubled, do you, Sam? You close yourself off. You brood. Do you really care about anyone?"

Durell replied thoughtfully, in a low voice, through the evening shadows that had crept into the room: "If the U.S. loses Dhubar's oil, it will be crippled. My job is to do whatever I can to prevent that. All I care about right now is my job."

His eyes followed her as she rose from the bed and stood before the balcony windows. She had a straight, firm figure that was proud, and Durell admired it against the sprawl of the capital city with its new boulevards, planted in the center with young tamarisks and spiny palms, lined with five- and six-story apartment and office buildings. Crowded mud-brick shops and tenements, the smoke of burning dung and sticks rising from them, huddled in a maze of alleys and side streets. On the western fringe stood the new National Assembly building and various modernistic government offices, their spaces cool behind honeycomb screens that hid glass walls. Most of the government buildings had spacious curbed yards, but grass did not grow there yet, and the yards were littered with sunbaked gravel where sand rats played.

Dara spoke quietly. "I had felt so close to you, since—since this morning. Now I feel all alone."

"Then you feel like the professional you're supposed to be," Durell said. "You know the rules: no emotional responses."

"I can play by them; do I sound upset?"

"You sound fine," Durell said.

"Good. Now—you come and look and let's see how you sound."

The flat challenge of her voice tripped alarms all over Durell's nervous system. Looking quizzically into her taut face, he strode to the window and stared out, beyond the Xs of masking tape.

In the middle of the city was a large, tin-roofed bazaar. The string of fires indicated that the riots had spread from there.

Now, on the boulevard about two blocks from the hotel, was the mob.

Chapter 7

"Maybe they're headed for the palace," Dara said.

"They won't make it; the streets are cordoned off with armor down there."

"It will shunt them right toward us," Dara said.

Durell's eyes swept to the floodlighted palace, where it rose above the old harbor basin, then back to the avenue before the hotel. Flames splashed across a shop front, and tongues of gasoline-fed fire rippled onto the sidewalk and dribbled into the gutter.

"Molotov cocktails," Durell said.

The mob spilled onto the thoroughfare from side streets and alleys, streams parting and recombining, their rumble growing to thunder beyond the thick panes of the hotel windows. Chants and cries of defiance punctuated the night. The skinny saplings in the center of the boulevard shuddered and swayed as the human tide rolled past them. In the first wave were white banners. Durell could not read them at this distance, but he guessed they were painted with more slogans against the Thirteenth Princess.

Dara's face was grim as Durell gazed through her reflection on the glass.

Fires sprung up from buildings on either side of the avenue as the mob advanced. The wind hurled sparks out over the swirling flood of humanity. Smoke looked white by the light of street lamps.

Two truckloads of troops sped down from the direction of the palace to aid a handful of police who struggled ineffectually to contain the destruction. The soldiers ran from the trucks and formed a firing line across the width of the avenue as their officers gestured and shouted against the mob's roar. Night had fallen now. Street lamps, the sultry flicker of burning shops and the flare of blazing automobiles lighted the scene.

Bottles and stones crashed and skittered around the troops.

Grenade launchers bucked and tear gas canisters burst in stinging white swirls, but the mob surged on, frenzied now.

The reluctant command to fire came too late. Rifles cracked and spat. Forms toppled but others took their places as hysterical rage generated suicidal determination, carrying the surging, bellowing mass over the disorganized and disintegrating line of soldiers.

Shrieks of terror and shouts of triumph mingled immediately in front of the hotel. Then the lights went out.

"Come on." Durell grabbed Dara's hand, twisted for the door.

"I didn't think they'd get this far." Her voice sounded forlorn in the darkness. She stumbled and gasped and caught her balance against Durell's shoulder.

He threw open the door and ran down the hallway toward a red emergency exit light that still glowed over the stairwell door. Dara's feet were a quick, light sound against the carpet. The taint of smoke came up the stairwell, and he concluded the rioters had fired the lobby, which had been partly burned the night before. Dara stayed with him as he took the steps two, three at a time, barely able to see by the dim red lights. They came out in a rearward angle of the lobby, where men looked like demons as they shattered windows and lamps and hurled anything they could lift onto a bonfire that raged in the center of the room.

There was a shout from behind Durell's field of vision, and Dara cried, "Sam!" He spun about just in time to see her swing and ax a thin, mustached man in the throat with the edge of her hand. He hit the floor on his knees, gagging and clawing for air, and she clouted his temple with the point of her shoe, and he lay still.

A rumble of feet came from the other direction. Durell twisted, and his .38 came into his hand in the same motion. There were four or five of them, shadows against the hot flames in the central lobby. He fired over their heads, the sound of the gun hollow and heavy in here, and they scattered and ran away, hands flailing in fright.

Durell pushed Dara through the outer door, his back against her, his gun covering the insane confusion of the lobby, and then they were outside, scrambling down the stony slope that met the beach.

They did not speak. Their breaths came in harsh pumpings. The sound of the surging, ranting mob was unreal, back there behind the hotel. It was the roar of storm waves on a granite headland. It dwarfed the plash of little combers out of the gulf. The grit tugged at Durell's heels as he ran, and he was aware of the swish of Dara's skirt, the chuffing of her breath. They came to a large stone groin, and he pulled her down in its shadow. The galaxy above was silver dust on velvet. Five hundred yards back down the beach, the modern hotel, part of an international chain, was a great, dark cube. Flames licked greasily, full of dark whorls of smoke, in the glass-enclosed lobby. Smoke came through shattered windows and was shredded by the wind. A machine gun stuttered. The wrenching growl of a tank or half-track came from somewhere. Durell heard a siren.

He peered toward the palace. Everything looked quiet in that direction. He smelled shellfish and brine in the damp corner between beach and groin, where the tide had fallen.

"The reception may have been cancelled," Dara said. She was next to him, trembling slightly.

"I doubt it; Sheik Zeid is a gutsy little guy."

"Should we go on to the palace, then?"

"Let's wait a bit." He surveyed the area of the hotel. The howl of the mob was receding. Gunfire echoed dimly from a distance. Beyond a string of street lamps, where horseshoe bats whirred through the light, picking off beetles and moths, red lights flashed and sent reflections across the facade of the hotel. Firemen had arrived to douse the blazing lobby.

His gaze slid back to the old harbor, just beyond the groin. From the near corner jutted a small boat basin, cramped with dozens of pleasure craft. A semicircular breakwater protected the harbor, which threw back long ribbons of reflected light from its still waters. Dhows of all sizes and conditions were moored along the breakwater, and others were tied up at new wooden piers and the bulkheaded shore.

Dara followed his gaze, and said: "Major Rabinovitch is supposed to be aboard the *Nedji.* I hope he made it."

"Let's go find out," Durell said.

"How do you like her?" Major Rabinovitch asked Durell.

"Looks seaworthy—especially if you can get the cockroaches to bail."

The Israeli spy chief's bitter eyes lighted with amusement, and a pleasant, soft-edged chuckle came from deep between his bullish shoulders. There was pride in his face, as he said: "We picked her up near Suez in the Yom Kippur melee. She was running supplies to Egypt's trapped Third Army." He looked around the small poop. "She's a sturdy vessel, the type the Arabs call a *zarook,* built in Yemen, lean and fast. She's been running the monsoon trade routes, Kuwait to Zanzibar, the last couple of years, hauling dates and mangrove poles and monitoring the Arabs' communications as the need arose. She was moored in Bahrain when the feathers hit the fan here."

The major was dressed in the white, nightshirtlike gown customary with Arab sailors. Chaim, the *nakhoda,* or master, far outshone him in a short sarong gathered at the waist and a gold-cloth vest. A Moroccan-born Jew, Chaim was as swarthy and aquiline as any Arab. He stood watch now, outside the small cabin where Durell, Dara, and the major talked.

Although the *Nedji* had a marine diesel engine for auxiliary power and a gasoline-run generator for her communications equipment, Rabinovitch preferred to maintain the look of an ordinary dhow as much as possible, so only a gimbaled kerosene lantern furnished light in the stuffy room.

He addressed Dara: "I'm only here to get the operation established, then I will be replaced by your permanent contact." He ran a finger beneath his lower lip. "We'll want to settle on a routine but avoid setting a pattern. You'll report to me daily, various times and places as I decide. I'll move the *Nedji* into the gulf and transmit to Israel twice a week, unless there's something more urgent. We'll avoid radio communications from the harbor, so that they can't triangulate us."

"Very well," Dara said, her hazel eyes brassy in the lantern-glow. "What about tonight?"

"Report to me here, after you leave the palace. I'd like an immediate reading on Sheik Zeid and his wife."

Durell broke in. "I hope to have Princess Ayla out of here tonight or tomorrow. She won't do you much good."

Major Rabinovitch turned his bulldoggish face back to Dara. "Nevertheless, see how close to her you can get."

"I understand," Dara replied. Her eyes switched to Durell, but they told him nothing before turning back to the major. "All embassy dependants have been evacuated," she said. "The princess has a Western background and may be lonely."

"Excellent," Rabinovitch replied.

"I don't like your emphasis on the princess," Durell said in a blunt tone.

"She's central to the whole problem, at the moment," the major shot back. Then, collecting himself, he spoke more calmly: "As I told you in London, Dara can be of great assistance in helping you"—again he hesitated before pronouncing the word—"*remove* Princess Ayla from the limelight."

"And, as I told you, the princess must not be harmed. There's a long-range relationship with Sheik Zeid that must be kept in mind."

Major Rabinovitch held out his palms. "I don't disagree with you, Cajun." Then he looked at Durell from under his shaggy brows and added: "But there are times when we must stamp out a fire and worry about the singed toes later."

"You'll have more than singed toes to worry about, Major," Durell said, his blue eyes darkening.

Rabinovitch straightened and spoke curtly: "You will allow Dara to be introduced as your wife, as per your orders?"

"I'll play along, for now," Durell said, aware of the moan of the wind in the dhow's coconut-fiber rigging, "but there's something else you should know. I've been reminded since arriving here that a Dhubaran specialty item is pink pearls out of the Persian Gulf. The man who tried to kill me in London wore a pearl like that. It could be only coincidence—"

"Or it could mean that somebody here has had a line

on you from the beginning," Major Rabinovitch supplied. His broad cheeks hardened. "But who?"

Dara stared at the lamp as if it were a crystal ball. "Start with Sam's friend, Princess Nadine," she said and turned to the two men. "If she told a single other person that she had requested Sam for this assignment, it could be all over the Mideast by now."

She and the major stared at Durell with something akin to apprehension. He knew they were calculating the odds against them, if they remained in his presence.

"You can terminate your operation now," he said evenly. "I keep moving either way."

"We still might get Dara planted safely," Rabinovitch said. "We're too close to stop now."

"If I were you, then, I'd be ready to get this tub out of here fast," Durell said.

"I am." The major's eyes went stony. "But we're counting on staying."

Chapter 8

The sound of gunfire still disturbed distant quarters of the city as Durell and Dara walked to the palace, about four blocks down the bay front. An orange glow shone against the star-laden sky where shops burned near the tin-roofed *souk* in the center of town. The curfew seemed fully effective in the vicinity of the palace. The only life on the street was a stray dog sniffing the dusty gutter, and it tucked its bony tail between its legs and ran away as they approached. Then the street curved around, and Durell saw automobiles stacked up before the palace, awaiting admission through its gate. A large plaza fronted the floodlighted palace, and it was ringed with troops and armored cars. In the dim further corners squatted French-made AMX–13 light tanks with short 75 mm. guns aimed down the side streets.

The couple was challenged immediately, showed their papers, and were ushered through the gate. There they joined the diplomats, some in striped pants, others in business suits or expensive Arab garb, and were led through a traditional triple-arched entrance. They came into a vast reception hall, where water gurgled from marble fountains and rose petals floated. Guards in blue and gold *ghutras* stood among the sofas and overstuffed chairs that were upholstered with blue brocade and gold thread. The air was frigid.

Durell had a sense of being hunted.

He felt a surge of urgency to complete his task before he was found.

He surveyed the mumbling crowd with calmly alert eyes, aware of the chill of Dara's hand where it rested in his. There was the American ambassador, a thin, grandfatherly figure with a cap of distinguished silver hair. A man who had not bought his appointment with political contributions but had worked his way up through the foreign service, he was one of those rarities: a diplomat with good marks in K Section's files. Across the room, the Russian ambassador, known to be a colonel in the KGB, chatted with his British counterpart. Representatives of many smaller nations were absent, but none of the earth's powers—including the Chinese, Japanese, West Germans, and French—overlooked this tiny desert sphere which a decade previously had been utterly insignificant.

A pair of guards wearing immense, gold-hilted scimitars carried gold incense burners into the big chamber, and Sheik Zeid was announced. He entered in swishing robes, his frank, sensitive face benevolent—for the moment, Durell thought. The dark and beautiful Princess Ayla captured all eyes a step behind. Her Turkish bodyguard, Yilmaz, loomed over her. Following them was a retinue of thirty or forty court functionaries and hangers-on, nearly all of them desert chieftans who wore stiff sandals and

sheer, elegant *thaubs* and hennaed their palms and out-
lined their eyes with charcoal.

In the forefront was Prince Tahir, tall and incongruous
in his tailored London suit, but seeming perfectly at ease
there near the center of things, Durell noted.

He did not look like a man who would willingly re-
linquish power, once gained, and Durell guessed that he
savored his influence with the sheik who loved his daughter.

As toasts in orange juice were being offered—alcoholic
beverages being forbidden by the Koran—Dara told
Durell: "Prince Tahir's baby girl doesn't look scared to
me. She looks cool as sherbet."

"I just hope Nadine got in touch with her," Durell said.

A reception line was formed, and Durell and Dara
moved step by step toward the ruling couple. "Got everything in place?" Durell asked.

Dara shot him a sidewise glance. "You should know,"
she said.

"Mr. and Mrs. Samuel Cullen Durell." A protocol
officer's announcement sent the pair across a small space
to where Sheik Zeid and Princess Ayla stood on an
enormous Kerman rug.

"How do you do, Mr. Durell?" Sheik Zeid spoke in
perfect English, his voice surprisingly deep and resonant.

"Salam alaikum," Durell said.

Zeid smiled and made the mandatory reply: *"Wa
alaikum as-salam."* The ritual greeting finished, he continued in his native tongue: "You speak Arabic, Mr.
Durell?"

"I have been favored with a knowledge of your language, Your Highness."

"I believe you are a friend of our Colonel McNamara?"

"Yes."

"It was he who introduced me to my wife."

"Allah karim, God is generous," Durell responded
politely.

"He is a good man, do you not think?" The emir's eyes
were just shiny masks.

"Of course, Your Highness—but troubled."

"We all are troubled. It is the times. We must not falter

in our resolve." A sharp edge of angry authority cut through his polite tone. "Traitors and spies must be dealt with severely."

Durell felt cold fingers yank at his guts, but he kept his face noncommittal. He wondered how much Sheik Zeid knew—and if it were *he* who had sent the assassin to meet him in London.

The sheik continued: "I do not believe anyone has informed me as to your purpose here, Mr. Durell."

"I am an expert on evacuations, Your Highness," he replied quickly. "As you know many of my countrymen are employed in your oil fields."

"Ah." A nod, a fixed, throughtful stare, then: "Let us hope that your skills need not be employed." He turned to the next person in line.

Princess Ayla, long ebony hair piled high on her head, resplendent in a white satin gown, looked every inch a queen. Her sensuous lips had the same quirk as her father's, a slightly downward twist to one corner of the mouth, as if impatient or petulant. It gave her a sulky charm, Durell thought, but in later years, as the flesh around the lustrous eyes and cheeks hardened, the trait might simply make her look cruel.

"Princess Nadine sends her love," he said as he took her hand.

Princess Ayla smiled, her neck rigid: "Our mother has spoken of you," she said in Americanized English that jarred with the regal pronoun.

"Recently, I trust?"

"Today—she recommends your friendship highly."

Durell felt relieved. At least Nadine had done her part of the job and laid the groundwork. He said: "Perhaps later I may speak with you alone—?"

"Ah! And this is Mrs. Durell!" Princess Ayla turned firmly away from him, making no reply, and warmly grasped Dara's hand.

At least he had planted the seed, he thought as he was forced to move on. Maybe she had cut him off to maintain secrecy in this chamber full of ears. Maybe she would contact him later, he decided, aware that

Prince Tahir's piercing stare followed him across the room.

He had no way of knowing what went on behind Princess Ayla's lovely face, but it would be easy, thinking of Prince Tahir, for a woman of her ancestry and rearing to be overwhelmed by dynastic compulsions. Through her and her alone, Ottoman blood once more shared a throne. The domain was small, Durell considered, but it was fabulously wealthy. And in those riches, siphoned in from the rest of the world in immense oil payments, lay power of untested dimensions.

He concluded it would take more than the rabble in the street to frighten her away from that.

His only hope was that she would leave for her husband's sake, but he had to weigh the alternatives if she refused, and his eyes went to the eager, deadly Dara.

Then his ear caught the shrill of a siren over the polite chatter of conversation that filled the ornate hall. He pushed aside a heavy velvet curtain and peered through French doors. An enormous garden was out there and at least a platoon of soldiers, barely visible in the starlight. They lounged idly, rifles slung, the orange coals of cigarettes glowing against their patient, fatalistic Bedouin faces. Behind them a high wall blocked the city from view.

The curtain swung back into place as Durell removed his finger and turned his eyes back to the chandeliered chamber. He saw Dara a few paces away now and surrounded by admiring courtiers and diplomats. The reception line still moved before Sheik Zeid and Princess Ayla, while Yilmaz hulked behind them, his olive face swinging mechanically back and forth over the gathering, eyes never resting.

Dara broke free of the huddle of men and sauntered to his side. "I couldn't *breathe,*" she said. She fanned herself.

Durell smiled. "You and the princess seemed to hit it off well."

"I have an invitation to brunch tomorrow—provided there *is* a tomorrow."

"Did she doubt there would be?"

"She must, if she's human."

"She may not be, by our standards—the queen bee isn't just a bee. Anyhow, we're in luck—you may be the only woman in the city she can relate to."

"Don't forget my brilliance and cunning, dear; it wasn't easy to get the invitation."

"I'll see you get a medal," Durell said in a dry voice.

"You're invited, too."

"I'll see you get two medals." He glanced swiftly around the room, satisfied to leave.

Dara touched his arm. "Sam—I don't trust her. There's something—something about those eyes."

Durell rolled his lip under, tasted salt from the beach. "Don't look now," he said, "but those eyes are drilling right into the back of your head. From the way they look, I'd say you're not the only one concerned about trust." He blew through his nose and said: "Let's call it a night."

They left the palace and walked along the bay-front street, the scrape of their footsteps coming back at them from the walls, warehouses, and mud-brick tenements. Yemenis and Sudanese, immigrants, inhabited the cheap, unsanitary housing now. Little Dhubar had a crippling labor shortage and had imported them to dig ditches and toil on the docks while most of its citizens took the better-paying oil-field jobs or engaged in commerce. The air was hot and humid after the crisp coolness of the air-conditioned palace, and Durell felt sweat beginning to prickle at his neck.

Dara was light as a shadow against his arm, her hair frosted by the glow of distant street lamps, her face serious. "Sam, I'm more concerned than ever, now that I've met Princess Ayla," she said.

"What do you mean?"

"The way she cut you off, and. . . ." Dara thought a moment. "I tried to bring up conditions here—her situation—but she simply would not discuss it. I have a feeling she's hiding something."

"There's nothing concrete to base that on."

"No, but that hook in your jaw you mentioned in the hotel?"

"Yes?"

"I hope Princess Ayla didn't just see it, somehow."

The wind had increased to a fresh breeze that stirred Dara's hair and shattered reflections on the bay with the small waves it made. A clang of buoys sounded from the Dhubar channel. The stench of burnt things came on the breeze and touched Durell's nose, but there was no sound of gunfire now. An eerie quiet shrouded the city.

Durell was aware of worry gnawing at the back of his mind. His voice was low and coarse, as he told Dara: "I must get her out of the country tomorrow."

"What if she won't go?"

"She's got to."

"You're making it difficult and dangerous, Sam."

"Yes?"

"You're exposing yourself, trying to be gentle." She watched his face, but he showed no response.

They walked on in silence. Durell glanced back over his shoulder. The street was dark, except for puddles of light beneath the widely separated streetlamps. The wreckage of a charred bus blocked an intersection that was strewn with broken glass and stones.

Dara's voice was abruptly argumentative. "You'll have to use force," she said.

"How much force?"

"As much as necessary."

"Even to killing her?"

"Maybe that's best—do I surprise you?"

"No."

She became more eager. "What do you think of it? We can pull it off, working together."

"No."

"The Ottomans held Israel once, too. I don't trust them. Maybe they want their old empire back. Israel would be on the list."

Durell spoke flatly. "Dhubar isn't a military threat to anybody. Its army is strained to provide internal security."

As if she had not heard him, Dara said: "I'll do it. At the brunch. You stay away."

"You're crazy. They'll tear you limb from limb."

"I don't care."

"You're under my orders. It's you who will stay away tomorrow."

They had stopped in the darker shadows of a warehouse, and they stared stubbornly at each other, Dara's eyes raised defiantly to his.

"Israel is a sovereign state," she spat. "I have to consider its security first."

Durell pushed her roughly back against the corrugated metal wall of the building. He shoved his fist in front of her eyes, suddenly grown round. He growled: "This is sovereign here. You will do whatever I say."

He expected a knee aimed at the groin or a chop to the neck, but he was not prepared for her complete turnabout, as she replied meekly: "Yes, Sam. Whatever you say."

"Do I have your word on it?" He held her by the shoulders.

"I promise, Sam."

He could not fully believe her even as her thin, sensitive lips closed over his, and she pressed hungrily against him. "Maybe I'm trying to impress you," she murmured. "I—I've been all confused since this morning."

"Then just do as I tell you," Durell said.

"You're the most exciting man I've ever known."

"Just don't get out of line."

He accompanied her to the pier where Major Rabinovitch waited in the *Nedji* and offered to go with her to the *zarook,* but she told him it was better if she went alone this time. He gave her that courtesy, reasonably sure she could take care of herself, and watched for a moment as she strode away, a lithe, supple shadow in the night. He thrust his hands into the pockets of his slacks, still troubled by Dara, and twisted his head around to the way he had come. The dark odor of the oil field came to him even here, standing over the water. He might have heard something over the soughing of the breeze, the low crash of small combers against the breakwater. He listened again as the water snapped and chimed at the pilings beneath his feet. Nothing.

He looked for Dara, but she had vanished from sight.

He pulled a breath and started for the hotel, roweled by the need for urgent action, aware of a sense of impending disaster that he seemed helpless to prevent.

A few minutes later, a pair of police officers wearing pistol lanyards under their epaulets detained Durell at the entrance to his hotel, reminded him of the curfew, and asked politely why he was breaking it.

He told them he had attended the emir's reception at the palace and produced his papers.

"You have a diplomatic passport, I see."

"I am a diplomat." Durell watched their faces. They were unremarkable in any way.

"Very well." He was waved into the burned-out lobby.

It was a grotesque mess. Its plate-glass walls lay on the floor, heaps of bright splinters in water that swam with the aftermuck of fire—char and dead embers, bits of plastic melted and twisted, scorched stationery, soggy newspapers, and black-quilled masses of singed furniture stuffing. The place reeked of burned plastic and varnish, and even a little wood, clear up to Durell's floor, although the blaze had been confined to the lobby.

The door to his room stood open.

He pulled his pistol and slid in sideways, thumbed the light switch and surveyed the destruction with impassive eyes. Obscenities and threats scrawled on the wall made it apparent that the vandals had singled out his room. The mattress had been slashed, the mirror over the dressing table looked as if it has been smashed with a rifle butt, and everything that could be moved had been turned topsy-turvy. Clothing from his and Dara's suitcases was strewn everywhere.

He kicked open the bathroom door. More wreckage.

He regarded the damage and considered his predicament. Obviously his cover had been blown, but that did not surprise him, not after London. Whoever came here had hoped to catch him and leave his body vandalized beyond recognition, just as they had this room. He shook the image out of his mind and concentrated on the next step as the pulse thudded against his temples and alarms jangled dimly in his mind.

He must get out of the hotel immediately, of course.

He decided he would go to the dhow and spend the night there, and tomorrow he would arrange for other quarters. . . .

He swung back to the bedroom, thinking he'd heard something, the shudder of the elevator, perhaps, or merely the sob of the wind.

Gun in hand he stooped about the room and snatched his and Dara's belongings from the floor and tossed them onto the ripped bedding, his mind going back to the Thirteenth Princess. With luck he would have her out of the country by nightfall tomorrow. Then crews paid with K Section funds would steal through the city in the early morning hours and nail up posters that announced the hated Turkish princess had fled. The posters were already printed—and bore the stolen imprimatur of a printing house known to favor the radicals.

The population would be unlikely to support further violence against the emir alone.

Durell threw the accumulated clothing into the suitcases indiscriminately, thinking it could be sorted out later, and glanced once more about the room.

They would be back, he thought.

If not in an hour, then in two.

There came a banging at his door.

Chapter 9

Durell's face snapped toward the door.

His forefinger felt oily on the trigger of his revolver as he stood stock-still. He did not speak. The wind purred out on the balcony. Seen from the corner of his vision, drilling rigs beyond the fringe of the city sparkled with strings of lights, and the new desalinization plant was a nest of pearls to the south.

The knock came again.

Durell moved swiftly and silently to the wall beside the door and doused the lights.

"Mr. Durell, sir?" The words conveyed an Arabic accent.

"Enter." Durell unlatched the door, but remained flush with the wall, his arm cocked, his pistol barrel pointed at the ceiling.

A sheet of light fell from the corridor into the room, and Durell reached suddenly and got a handful of the man's collar. The other resisted only weakly as Durell spun him to the floor and knelt on his chest, a grip on his throat, the gun at the point of his nose.

"What brings you? Speak!" Durell hissed in Arabic.

"Don't shoot, sir!" The man gasped against the pressure of Durell's knee, speaking with broken breaths, wide eyes fixed on the muzzle of the gun.

"Then tell me your purpose." Durell gave a twist to the man's collar and saw his cheeks bloat darkly. "Quickly, now."

"Princess Ayla—"

"Princess Ayla what?"

"Oh, sir! The princess sends a message."

"Let's have it, then." Durell's voice was a soft menace. Without ceremony he yanked the man from the floor and shoved him against the wall, banging his head so that it rocked. Then he stepped away, being careful to keep the man covered, closed the door, flipped the light switch, and regarded his catch. He was an Arab of middling size, and wiry, but there was no fight in his white-ringed eyes and he seemed to have swallowed his tongue. His fine wool *thaub,* with its border of silver embroidery, marked him for a man of some consequence, and Durell guessed he had not seen the business end of a revolver many times in his life.

"What's the message?" Durell demanded.

The man swallowed, and his hands fiddled nervously

with his beard. "Yes, sir. Princess Ayla says you are to meet her at the Mobarek Mosque, in the courtyard there."

Durell's pulse quickened. "When?"

"Half an hour."

"Very well." Durell pushed his revolver into the frightened man's belly. "You come, too."

The man's eyes bugged beneath his *ghutra* with its black-corded *agal,* and his fingers twiddled an invisible lute of fear. "But I must return to Her Highness. She awaits word of your compliance. She will not leave until she has it."

Durell's jaw muscles knotted as he tried to read the man's face. "Go, then," he said.

The Arab darted for the door, his breath rasping against a terror-constricted throat.

Durell pushed the snub-nosed pistol into his waistband and waited as a few moments ticked by. He wished he might have taken the man with him: he would have served as hostage and shield, might even have warned Durell of an ambush for fear of his own life.

If someone were trying to lure him into a trap, the strategy had been thought out with the precision of a chess master.

The princess would not come, they said, unless the messenger returned. Which meant that Durell must walk into the unknown alone.

He took the elevator down and found that crews had arrived to clean the lobby and make temporary repairs. Plywood sheeting was going up over broken windows, but the warm, sultry wind still whistled through and brought the scents of dust and imported Persian charcoal, of animal pens and oil-field gas. Trash barrels sat about, loaded with debris. Water was being swept out and mopped up. With the plywood shutting off light from the street and the dim glow of only two or three serviceable lamps, the big space was gloomy as an underground bunker.

Durell glanced at his wristwatch as he strode briskly to a row of telephone booths. It was almost midnight. He fed change into an instrument and waited impatiently as it rang, his eyes ranging back and forth across the lobby. Only hotel employees seemed to be about. When a receiver was lifted at the other end of the line, he asked for a military attaché at the U.S. embassy. "Well, wake him up," he said in a tone of stifled anger. And then:

"Major Mills? Sam Durell. Yes. Where's Task Force Talon?"

"On station in the Persian Gulf. Arrived approximately one hour ago."

"Get me a chopper. Immediately."

"Where do you want it?"

"Just a minute." Durell reached inside the sleeve of his jacket and withdrew from the lining a piece of blue flimsy that was folded in a square chip. He flicked it open and smoothed it against a telephone directory and studied the finely detailed map of Dhubar City that had been drawn over a grid on it. He held his fingertip on one of the squares, and said: "Coordinate twenty-three. The Mobarek Mosque. In the courtyard."

"Roger," the major said, his tone crisp. "How about I include a squad of leathernecks?"

"Thanks, major, but my job is to prevent a war, not start one," Durell said and hung up.

As he strode out of the hotel, he saw a look of wonder in the eyes of the cleanup crew. Only a *kaffir*—an infidel—fool would go out there tonight, they were thinking.

He almost bumped into Dara, who returned from the *Nedji* with hurried footsteps. He took her arm and held her in the shadows, and said: "Our room isn't safe. Don't even go in the hotel. You can call for your luggage later."

"What happened?" The breeze flipped a yellow curtain of hair across a cheek, and she tossed her head.

"They trashed the room." Durell sucked an angry breath.

"They? Who?"

"Someone." Durell shook his head. "I don't know. Come on."

"Where are you going?"

"To get the Thirteenth Princess." Durell stepped away.

"You're joking." Dara caught up with him.

"If there's a joke, it's on me. We'll find out. But watch yourself."

The wind fluttered her dark dress against the soft turnings of her legs as they moved into the street, crossed the thoroughfare, and turned into a side street. There was no good excuse for breaking the curfew now, and Durell hoped fervently to avoid the military and police patrols that roamed the city. In this narrow byway the starlight crusted the nearly windowless mud buildings with a leaden efflorescence, and sand blew from the rainspouts. The falling sand made a thin, spattering sound against tin awnings here and there, and paving stones polished by generations of calloused feet held the sand in soft puddles.

Dara's breathing came light and quick beside him. "How did you arrange it?" she questioned.

"The princess? She must have had a change of heart. She sent for me."

"Sam, wait." Dara stopped, her face wan and troubled. "Do you know what you're walking into?"

"Do I have a choice?"

Dara did not say anything.

They had no difficulty finding the mosque. The glazed tiles of its onion-bulb dome sparkled against the ultramarine sky. Durell regarded its arched portal with care as they strolled past, then they turned to pass it again.

"I don't see a courtyard," Dara said.

"It will be behind the building." Durell looked up and down the street. "There's a high wall back there. We'll have to go through the inside of the mosque."

A scout car snorted into the narrow street, bumping and lurching over the paving stones, and Durell jerked Dara into a doorway. He waited until the patrol had passed, waited half a minute more, ducked into the mosque.

They moved soundlessly across prayer rugs arranged on a worn, limestone floor. It was cool in here. Pigeons roosting in the dome made guttering noises, and half a dozen large clocks that stood around the elaborately tiled

walls clicked and clacked. Wrought-iron chandeliers
shaped like wagon wheels hung on long ropes, but the
only light was a muted glow from the area of the Moorish-
columned *mihrab* and *minber*.

He tested the latch on a blue-painted plank door, a
thin ribbon of light gleaming on the barrel of his gun,
held down by his thigh. The door was unlocked. It
groaned a little as he pushed it open with two fingers.
He flagged Dara to a halt and listened and sniffed the
still air for the scent of a cigarette or perfume or anything
out of the ordinary. Only a musty odor teased his nose.
There was almost no light in there, the only illumination
coming from a narrow window high to the left, above a
flight of stone steps worn hollow by ages of use. The
gusty breeze made sounds like an enormous towel being
thrown again and again at the dome of the building.
Quickly he stepped through, Dara coming behind, and
found a second door and slid silently into the courtyard.

It was a confusion of star-frosting and shadows, black
on gray.

No one called. Nothing moved.

Dara reached into the bodice of her black dress, and
the silver derringer shone in her hand.

"You take one side, and I'll take the other," Durell
said.

They parted, moved down two sides of the arcaded
courtyard wall. Shadows behind the columns were dense.
Water tinkled from a fountain in the center of the courtyard and fell into a pool impounded by low, circular
walls decorated with arabesque tiles. There were aloes,
fig and orange trees, a large grape arbor. Crickets
chirruped and mosquitoes whirred angrily against the flute
notes of a *bulbul* that sang in the shrubs.

There was no sign of the Thirteenth Princess.

No one was in the courtyard.

"What now?" Dara asked.

"She may have been delayed."

"I don't like this."

Durell's voice was low and patient. "We'll wait."

The wind swept against the dome and minarets and

fell into the courtyard and stumbled weakly among the trees there. A roof-mounted air-conditioning unit purred somewhere nearby. Durell thought of the navy helicopter, shone a penlight on his wrist chronometer. It was due soon.

He studied the gloomy courtyard, judged its dimensions, decided there seemed to be room for a landing on its south side, between the pond and arcade. It would be tight, and there was the wind to consider. The pilot must make the final decision after a look under his landing floods. If it could not be accomplished, a lowered sling would have to suffice.

Durell did not know what he would do if the princess refused to go. He dismissed the idea.

She had to go.

Dara stood next to him, almost military in her straight bearing and disciplined silence. They watched and listened as more minutes passed. Then Durell heard the dim flutter of the helicopter, still out over the gulf.

At the same moment a wooden groan announced the opening of the courtyard door.

Chapter 10

Durell hurried up the length of the courtyard, toward the mosque, aware of the brisk tap of Dara's feet on the stones of the arcade floor behind him. He thought he saw movement at the door up there, but the night shadows obscured everything. He slowed and moved closer, pistol ready. A sobbing gasp that came through the hollow moan of the wind stopped him dead in his tracks.

Then he bent slightly, crept forward, picked out the form of a huge man who struggled feebly to rise from the ground.

"Yilmaz!" Dara cried.

"He's been shot," Durell said with stifled dismay.

He knelt beside Princess Ayla's bodyguard. The man's shirtfront was sopping with blood, and the hand that he extended weakly toward Durell was streaked with blood that had run down his arm and dribbled from his fingertips. Durell struggled against a sense of defeat that rose in him as he cradled Yilmaz's massive head and loosened his tie.

"What happened?" Durell asked.

"Army—patrol. I ran. They—" The big Turk grimaced and clenched his eyes shut. His breath came in shallow, panting waves. Only an animal stamina had carried him this far, Durell decided, but he seemed less than half-conscious now, was on the point of giving up.

"Where is Princess Ayla?" Durell urged.

"I came to—" Blood bubbled in Yilmaz's words, and he coughed and widened his eyes. Durell waited. Something feral, cunning, hunted gathered in him to flee, but he denied it. Yilmaz licked his lips, smearing blood from his tongue, and gasped: "She—she left—"

The Turk stiffened as if jolted with electricity, and as suddenly went limp.

Durell and Dara exchanged stares.

"She played you for a sucker, Sam. She's out, but you're going to take the rap. You're—"

"Shut up."

"I'm just telling you."

"We don't know what happened."

Dara nodded toward the dead Turk, and wings of her short, blond hair fell past her cheeks. "You won't find out from that," she said.

The battering racket of the helicopter came abruptly from just beyond the walls, and Durell craned his face up to the sky. The naval helicopter banked into view, coming around the icy sheen of the dome of the mosque, and settled low and uncertainly toward the courtyard. Landing lights blasted away the darkness. There was a tornadic whirl of wind, and the shrill of jet turbines ripped the air as the chopper cozied into the only small space that would accommodate it.

Dust and sand raised by the spinning rotor blades choked and stung Durell as he ran for the machine, ripping through shrubs and hurdling benches. He banged on the cockpit door with the butt of his pistol. It swung open, and a helmeted crewman leaned into the wind and noise.

Durell shouted to be heard: "Tell the pilot—return to your ship."

The crewman made a face of incomprehension.

Durell spun his arm around and pointed to the sky.

The crewman nodded this time. "What about the passenger?" he called.

The wind stood Durell's thick black hair on end as he shook his head. "There isn't any," he yelled. "Just get the hell out of here."

The door snapped shut; the noise of the turbines rose to an earsplitting shriek; the craft lifted away.

In the comparative silence after its departure, Durell felt as if he had been abandoned at the bottom of a black abyss. He became aware of Dara at his side. She spoke in a tone of dread. "Something tells me it's going to be a long night, Sam."

Durell made no reply, but the sweat soaking his collar felt suddenly chill. He cast his gaze around the courtyard one more time, then entered the door Yilmaz had come through, stepping over the corpse that lay like a fallen tree. He pushed through the second door into the dimly lighted mosque, and headed for the street entrance.

He had taken only a couple of steps when he froze at the clatter of feet out there.

Then the Arab who had brought Princess Ayla's message to him burst into the mosque, aimed an accusing arm at Durell, and shouted: "That's him!"

The whole Dhubaran army seemed to be tumbling inside behind him.

"Halt! Halt!" an officer bellowed.

But Durell was back in the space between two doors and herding a momentarily confused Dara toward the stairs on the right. He heard the confused slap of many running feet as he stumbled over worn stone steps, righted himself, scrambled up past Dara, and tugged urgently at her hand. He could barely see in here. Now she followed the ring of his heels in the darkness, her breath gusty and light. Eight steps up he stopped at a landing, where the staircase doubled back and the night sky shone through a single high window. Dara ran into him, bounced off, started up the next flight, but he grabbed her and held her back. He studied the window, blood pounding in his ears, and seemed to be looking up from the black depths of a well. Then the soldiers hurtled through the iron-studded door below and through the second door and into the courtyard, and there was an immediate shout and hubbub as they found the body of Yilmaz.

Durell gritted his teeth and waited, pressed against the wall, holding Dara still. He heard a command in Arabic to scour the courtyard for the two foreigners, and then he breathed a little easier. They had a minute or two before the search returned to the interior of the mosque. He waited a few seconds, then led Dara on up the stairs to where he could just reach the window. He held Dara beneath the armpits and raised her light, svelte frame until she could catch the window sill and crawl through, and then he hauled himself up to follow. They came out on a narrow walkway that embraced the enormous, shining bulb of the dome. The wind whipped and tore at them. Lights of the city's modern office towers blazed over the mud and tile rooftops. Oil-field flares and rig lights winked in the distance. The harbor, viewed between the taller buildings, was a dark glass.

"We'll have to jump to the street," Durell told Dara. "They'll come back to the stairs when they don't find us in the courtyard. Can you do it?"

"Sure." She knelt and looked down into the alley.

"Just keep your knees loose."

"I know," she said impatiently. She lowered herself over the edge of the walkway, the breeze billowing her skirt to show flashes of white thigh. Her voice came as a strained whisper—"Here's hoping!"—and she let go. A soft thump and a gasp came back to Durell's ears, but nothing to indicate harm or fear, and then he turned loose, felt a rush of air and then the solid slap of the paving stones on the balls of his feet. He pitched, rolled, smacked into Dara, and came up in a tangle of arms and legs.

Quickly and soundlessly they moved toward the street, the rough plaster of the wall scraping their backs as they went sidewise in the shadows. Durell heard the commotion of the soldiers from above now, as the search for him went into the upper reaches of the mosque. He peered around the corner of the alley, into the street where two troop trucks loomed darkly. They were parked in front of the mosque, and a single guard walked to and fro beside them.

Durell signaled Dara to stay out of sight, waited until the guard had turned and was walking away, then hopped three long, silent strides to hide himself behind the tailgate of the first truck.

When the guard passed on his return, Durell hammered the hard edge of his palm against the nape of the man's neck, and the other dropped in his tracks. Durell caught him as he fell and dragged him into the alley and laid him down.

"Did you kill him?" Dara asked.

"I'm not asking for more trouble. He'll just have a stiff neck for a week or so."

"They will kill us, if they get the chance—they'll certainly kill me, if they find out—"

"Let's beat it," Durell interjected.

They ran to the nearest truck, hopped into the cab, and roared away.

"What will you do now?" Dara asked.

"Get to the American embassy, try to find out what the score is." Durell drove with one hand and wiped sweat from his brow with the other.

"I'm not sure I want to know the score." Dara's tone was sour. She held her lower lip between straight, white teeth.

"At least Princess Ayla's out of the country."

"Yes—and the army's after us. *We* should have got on that helicopter."

Durell did not bother to answer, his mind busy with other matters. He would have preferred to deal with a K Section Central here, but Dhubar was a newly important country in which his agency had no Central. It simply lacked the funds. The ambassador he must rely on, Norman Swayne, knew nothing of Durell's mission, only that he was a U.S. intelligence officer, and that he was to be given consideration and assistance. Such arrangements seldom worked well. The diplomats, fearful for their carefully cultivated relationships with the host country, viewed K Section operations with suspicion and trepidation. Men such as Durell, on the other hand, tended to play fast and loose with the rules and to rely as little as possible on a State Department that had its own aims and means of achieving them.

They came to a roadblock, were waved on, thanks to their military vehicle.

The city seemed as empty as the desert that pressed against it on three sides. The bark of a dog echoed down a barren, windy alley. A rat darted through the glare of the headlamps as the truck rumbled and jounced down a back street. The reek of dead fires was everywhere. Durell's wristwatch read one-thirty.

Dara spoke over the squeak and roar of the truck. "Did you ever stop to think what these people would do to me, if they found out I was a Jew?"

Durell glanced at the rear-vision mirror. "You knew when you volunteered to come here."

"It just seems that everything has fallen apart." She lowered her big hazel eyes toward her lap.

Durell had never seen her this depressed before. It worried him, and it annoyed him, but he decided to keep that to himself. He put an arm gently around her shoulders and pulled her next to him. "Don't waste your time thinking like that," he said. "Everything will come out all right."

"But what if it doesn't?" Her eyes turned defiant. "If they catch me, I'll kill myself."

Durell spared a glance from the road to try and judge if she were serious. "Are you that frightened of them?" he asked.

"Not frightened—I just won't give them the satisfaction of doing—the things they would do."

Durell saw a stubborn hatred on her freckled face, a hatred that would live beyond the grave, if such a thing could be. He thought then how little he really knew about this woman in the intimate pose of his wife. She was in her early twenties, spoke the American idiom like a native— which meant she must have been stationed there for some time. Her walk was a slightly but clearly prideful swagger, as if she were ready for any challenge. She had never shown real fear—not until she mentioned capture by the Arabs—and then it had been fear of humiliation and the violation of her pride more than of her body.

You couldn't talk about it to a person who felt like that, he thought. There was nothing to be said.

He peered ahead, down the dark, narrow street. "We'd better ditch the truck here and go on to the embassy afoot," he said.

"The situation is grave—very grave, Mr. Durell."

"Tell me what you have learned, Mr. Ambassador."

Norman Swayne touched his silver hair above the right temple, made a tent of his fingers and delicately cleared his throat. "The palace believes you took the princess."

"Go on."

"They believe you kidnaped her."

Durell's face hardened. "They are mistaken," he said.

"Are they? I must tell you, I've dealt with K Section personnel before." The ambassador's thin, dry lips smiled without amusement. "I found them capable of nearly anything."

"I did not kidnap the princess," Durell repeated firmly.

"I don't expect you to admit it to me, even if you did,

Mr. Durell." Swayne smiled politely at Dara. "Forgive me, Mrs. Durell. It's quite late, I know—would you care for coffee?"

"Thank you, no," Dara said. She looked a bit haggard, Durell noted, her short hair windblown; sandy, ocher smudges on her black dress. He sat with her on a low, sumptuously upholstered divan to one side of the sweeping, tidy vista of Swayne's desk. His chair was higher, so that he looked down on them, and Durell resented the cheap trick and felt not the least intimidated. From the monochrome yellow carpet to a Nineteenth Century painting of the Hudson River that dominated the walls, the office might as well have been in Denver as in Dhubar.

The ambassador straightened his tie and leaned toward them. Despite the late hour and Durell's unexpected arrival, he was impeccably dressed in an off-white suit with vest, soft white shirt, and club tie. His dark tan told Durell that he had spent a lot of time outdoors, probably at the new golf club with oil company executives or falconing and cruising to the Persian Gulf islands with his late friend, the old emir. "What are we going to do about this, Mr. Durell?" he said delicately.

"We'll see," Durell said. "What makes them think I kidnaped the princess?"

"It's rather painful for me to say."

Durell spoke with a wry drawl. "Give it a try."

"Yes. Well, they say your lovely wife"—he nodded graciously toward Dara—"is a Jew, an agent of the Shin Beth."

Durell tried not to show his sense of shock and alarm, but his efforts were wasted on the old ambassador, who just smiled—this time sincerely.

Dara handled it better. "Horseradish," she snorted.

The ambassador was amused. "I told them it was absurd, my dear."

"But you didn't believe it was absurd," Durell said.

"No." Swayne's eyes went steely.

"And they didn't believe it when you told them."

"No." The ambassador drew a deep, slow breath. "I'm afraid they wish to take you into custody. And Mrs. Durell as well."

"We have diplomatic immunity," Durell replied.

"Quite so."

Dara spoke, her voice thin and uncertain. "The worst they can do is deport us."

The ambassador peered at them from beneath his high forehead and shaggy, white brows. "Not—quite—so," he replied. He took another breath and looked up at the ceiling. "You see, we have an exceptional situation—let us say it is unique." He cut his cunning old eyes back at Dara. "The wife of the ruler of a nation has disappeared, is believed to have been the victim of foul play—she left her infant son behind; would she have done that voluntarily? And the ruler is consumed with anger"—Swayne lowered his voice—"and desire for revenge. Now. How might he vent this fury? He could embargo oil exports to the country he believed responsible—say a three-month hiatus, just a slap on the hand. But a dangerous display of power that would temporarily weaken us and possibly create an outcry for military intervention. That would make other Arab states—and more importantly, the Russians—very nervous. Someone could miscalculate, and. . . ." He lifted his frosty brows and held out his hands.

"Come to the point," Durell said.

"The point is, that could all be avoided—perhaps—if the Dhubaran government had an opportunity to question those parties it suspects."

"You mean us. You're asking us to give ourselves up. For something we didn't do." Durell's voice was harsh.

"If you're not guilty, what have you to fear? It would lift suspicion, and assuage Sheik Zeid's honor, at least vis-à-vis the United States." Slack skin tightened around the old man's eyes. "The situation is explosive, Mr. Durell. Which do you think more sensible: surrender yourself or perhaps start events toward disaster?"

"Neither," Durell said flatly.

Swayne's voice turned tough. "I shall have to query Washington, before I allow you to leave."

"I intend to find the princess, sir." Durell kept his face hard. "That's the only solution."

The ambassador's voice became more stubborn. "I'm sorry. I must detain you."

"Don't try it, sir. It would be messy." He rose and moved to the door, and Dara came up beside him and looked up at him and then back at the ambassador.

Her voice was bitter, as she told Swayne: "This is all so damnably laughable—but I suppose you wouldn't understand."

"I'm afraid I would not see the humor, Mrs. Durell." He slid his gaze to Durell. "I could call the guard."

Durell twisted the doorknob, looked into the empty hallway, then back. "I said I would find the princess. I'll get to the bottom of this. You have my word."

As he and Dara stepped out, Swayne said: "If you fail, the damage may be incalculable." And then, "Good luck."

"How will you find her, Sam? How?"

"I have a hunch she's flown to Istanbul," Durell told Dara.

"To be with her mother?"

"To hide until Dhubar cools off. She showed real affection for Nadine in the films we viewed in London. There's no one else for her to turn to."

The elevator did a slow bounce and opened its doors, and they turned into a long corridor. Durell showed his papers to a marine guard, and they went out of the building through a side exit. The crush of dead, stale heat rolled over them as they approached the street through a small garden of ornamental shrubs and small trees.

"Israel's stake in this is as big as your country's," Dara said. "I'm going to Turkey with you."

"I expected you would," Durell said.

"You won't try to stop me?"

"You've been wiped out here. I can hardly leave you behind," Durell said as he paused at an iron gate. He cast his eyes back and forth, up and down the dark and deserted street. The wind made boiling sounds in the short palms and acacias that grew in the little garden. "Let's get the truck," he said as he pushed the gate open.

"Do you think we can drive across the border?" Dara asked.

"We wouldn't have a chance." Durell kept walking. He could smell the odors of goat dung and urine mixed with the fragrances of jasmine and spices.

Dara spoke again through the gloom. "The airport will be under surveillance."

"We'll drive to the old harbor. We'll take the dhow," Durell said. "Once in the Persian Gulf, Task Force Talon will pick us up. If we miss it, we can still land in Iran. There won't be any problems there."

A twisting sense of urgency wound Durell's nerves taut. Every hour counted, but patience and slow caution would be necessary to get him out of Dhubar. The whole security establishment would be alerted, focused on one thing now:

Get Durell; get the Israeli spy he calls his wife.

They turned left, went a block, crossed an alley, and the truck came into view, cold starlight glinting on its cab. Suddenly Durell was staggered by an explosive, blinding glare, threw the shield of a hand before his eyes—saw that someone had turned on the truck's high beams. . . .

Chapter 11

"Oh, no!" Dara breathed, the two syllables running to-gether in a pinched sound of dismay.

From the corner of his eye Durell saw her hand lift abruptly toward the hidden derringer. He slapped it down, hoping he did so before the move caould be analyzed. "Don't be a fool," he said. "Save it."

There was no point in running, except to get shot down, Durell decided. Blank-walled mud buildings crowded in on the street here, their gritty facades shining and glittering in the fierce glare, and Durell sensed guns aimed at him. He might as well have been in an arena at high noon.

Pat McNamara's voice was hoarse with triumph, as he called above the wind. "You're under arrest, Durell. The lady, too. Don't move; stay cool; make it easy on yourself."

Durell raised his eyes above the stabbing dazzle of the headlamps and saw that the roofs on both sides of the street were lined with armed men.

"You're making a mistake, Pat," Durell called out. "They won't like this in Washington."

A crude laugh came from the direction of the truck, behind the lights. "Maybe not, but it'll play damn well here. That's all that counts." He showed himself against the brilliance of the headlamps, a heavy, slope-shouldered cutout that moved cautiously toward Durell. "The cops and the army are looking all over town for you, running around like crazy. I had an idea you'd come back here, though," he gloated. He lifted a chopped .45 Colt automatic, and lowered his voice. "I'm sorry it had to be this way," he said. "Real sorry."

"Can it." Durell's tone was blunt. "You can't play both sides. Anyhow, my guess is that you're tickled to death to do a big favor for Sheik Zeid and show him what a good boy you are."

McNamara's teeth shone in yellow light reflected from the mud walls, and he wiggled the .45. "Just drop your weapons," he said.

Durell's .38 clacked to the paving stones. He held his breath for Dara's derringer.

"I mean you, too, little lady," McNamara persisted. "We've got a computer file on you that goes back three years. I've known about you all along; I was just waiting for you to show your hand. Don't expect me to believe you're unarmed."

"I have no weapon," Dara said and stared at him with hateful eyes.

"Ali?" McNamara spoke to one of the men who had come down from the rooftops, and a subordinate with ropy muscles showing below the short sleeves of his shirt and an eager, sharp-featured face stepped forward. "Search her," McNamara said.

The man patted down the sides of her dress, turned to McNamara and shrugged.

McNamara cursed. "Get between her boobs, you idiot. This isn't a church social."

"Now just a minute. . . ." Durell began, as the man plunged a hand into Dara's bodice with obvious relish. A savage cry of disgust and fury sounded in Dara's throat as she slammed a knee into Ali's groin, and he went double and stumbled back with a twisted face. McNamara shouted something in Arabic, and other men darted into the radiance of the truck lights, grabbing and clawing at the struggling Dara, smothering her efforts with their combined strength. Durell heard a short scream, the abrupt tearing of dress material.

He caught the nearest man by the back of the neck and hurled him away, and the man hit the mud wall and slid down like a smashed egg. Durell waded into the midst of the men, surprised in the back of his mind that McNamara had not shot him—but then McNamara would want him alive—and lashed out with elbow, fist, foot, and knee. He saw Dara down on all fours, trying to get up, but jostled off-balance, rolled, kicked, and stepped on. Except for a bra, her glossy skin showed through a ragged rip in her dress that extended from neck to navel, and the little derringer holster that hung by a chain was empty—either someone else had the gun now or it was lost. Durell lunged, swung, and kicked, but the men were all over him like a pack of wolves, and blows rained on him from every direction, and he found himself borne down, tasting blood.

Then something cracked against the back of his head. Lightning flashed behind his eyes.

When it was gone, there was nothing.

Durell did not know how much time had passed, but he could not have been out long. He lay very still and waited for his mind to clear. First in his awareness was the jolting of the floor, but it wasn't a floor, he realized, hearing a laboring engine and the rumble of tires. It was the bed of a truck. Scrapes and bruises ached all over, and it felt as if an ax head was buried in his skull. With some effort, he collected himself and put aside the pains and torments. But one minor discomfort persisted, where something prickled annoyingly against his cheek. He just barely opened his eyes and saw a folded canvas awning, used to shelter troops from sun and rain. His face lay on a loose heap of hemp rope that would serve to tie the awning down.

He saw now that he had been tossed into the forward corner of the troop truck, where a slatted sideboard and headboard kept him from falling out.

Durell moved his head with nearly imperceptible slowness and kept the rest of his body lying loose, as it had fallen. Dara sat in the other forward corner of the truck bed, the wind whipping her straw-colored hair about her face, and held her torn dress together. Her wide mouth was compressed into a sullen line as she defiantly returned the stares of two leering guards. The guards sat on the tail end of the bed, one on each side, M–16s between their knees.

Durell noted thankfully that they were sparing little attention for him.

A plan had been growing in his mind since he had seen the rope. There wasn't much time to act, and it was a long shot, but it was all he had.

The truck lurched and banged, as he slowly and deliberately extended one arm through the slats of the headboard, reached down, unscrewed the cap to the gasoline tank, and dropped it. Next, counting on the darkness and skillful muscle control to conceal his efforts as much as possible, he snaked a length of the rope into the gasoline tank and let it soak there for a moment.

Dara saw that he was up to something, but the guards had not caught on. She engaged them in an exchange of name calling and obscenities that brought roars of laughter from the end of the shivering, rattling truck bed.

Carefully, Durell retrieved the dripping rope.

The last step could only be done openly. But if he were quick enough. . . .

He struck a match close to the rope. The match was blown out immediately, but the spark had been enough, and the rope turned into two feet of flaming wick. He lurched up, feeling the startled eyes of the guards on him and the grinding need for instant action. He dipped over the headboard and hurled the blazing rope into the driver's face. It gave him some pleasure that Ali was at the wheel.

There was an immediate lurch that threw the guards off balance, then a wild scream as fire flashed into Durell's vision, beyond the rear window. He dropped to his knees and hung onto the headboard with all his strength. The guards were not a source of worry on the crazily swerving vehicle.

"Hang on!" he yelled to Dara and saw fright in her wide, fixed eyes.

The truck slammed into a wall and caromed away in a cloud of grit, and one of the guards rolled off the bed and into the street as easily as a melon. Then there was a rending, stupefying crash. Mud bricks exploded in every direction. The remaining guard was hurtled the length of the bed and hit the headboard, splintering it with a sickening crunch.

Durell was half-dazed, although he had braced himself. He came to his senses with acrid smoke burning his nostrils. The driver screamed, whimpered, shrieked. He was trapped in the bent and twisted wreckage, and Durell glimpsed a flail of arms, then his blazing head and shoulders as he attempted to hurl himself out his window.

Durell scuttled over the sodden heap of the dead guard and slapped Dara's cheeks to revive her. She moaned as her long lashes fluttered. He did not think she was seriously harmed. Swiftly, he gathered up the guard's M–16 and dragged her to the rear of the bed.

He did not know what kind of building they had crashed

into. It was dark in here, except for the wavering patterns of light thrown through the dust and smoke by the crackling fire in the truck cab. At least there seemed no innocent casualties, he noted. The cavity of the broken wall beckoned escape.

He did not go that way.

Dara was on her feet now. The fire spread from the truck as he held her and studied her eyes.

"I'm all right," she said. Her voice was shaky.

The squeal of brakes sounded from the street. Car doors slammed. Men shouted.

Durell pushed through splintered and tumbled furnishings to the rear of the room and found a doorway. Smoke seared his lungs, and heat scorched his face.

"Hurry!" he yelled, as Dara stumbled through the debris after him.

He saw that the driver was still now and hung like a charred beam half out the window of the fiery cab. The stench of his cooked flesh brought spasms to Durell's throat as he went back impatiently to shepherd Dara to the rear.

Wails of terror and alarm came from upstairs.

Men called in the street.

A figure appeared in the toothed gap of the wall, wavering and indistinct viewed through the heat and flames, and there was a spitting racket of automatic rifle fire. The fire and smoke-filled room made sounds like a hornet's nest, and something nipped hotly across Durell's thigh. He crouched, shot from the hip, and saw the man out there flop backwards.

Then Durell and Dara were in the alley and ran for their lives.

After ten harrowing minutes of deadly cat and mouse, Durell and Dara came out of a maze of fetid alleyways. The sound of the chase was right behind them, harsh in their ears. Calls and the slap of running feet mingled with the bleat of awakened goats, the bray of a donkey.

Durell's nerves were raw. There could be no mistaking the consequences of capture now. Blood had been drawn, and only blood in return would satisfy. Pat McNamara would not be able to stop it, even if he wished.

Durell leaned around the corner of a building, glimpsed his hotel to the left, the palace to the right. The old harbor seemed a black void beyond the broad avenue. The wind blew against Durell's face and chilled the rivulets of perspiration. It smelled clean and briny as he filled his aching lungs.

Two blocks to the north, midway between where he hid and the floodlighted facade of the hotel, sat another of those Shorland armored cars. Troops were deploying from trucks parked in the hotel driveway, some moving away, others filing in his direction, their rifles held at port arms.

"McNamara must have called for help," Dara said. She seemed composed and eager now, despite the pressure.

"They're about to cordon us off," Durell replied. He looked back toward the approaching sounds of pursuit. "There's nothing to do but make a break for it."

"We didn't get this far to fail now," Dara said. She laid a long, slender hand on his arm.

He did not look at her but surveyed the boulevard. It would be impossible to cross, he thought, except for the miserly cover of a few scrawny trees and low shrubs that grew in the center strip. If that screened their approach across the first two lanes, then speed and surprise might get them safely across the second two. After that it would just be a rat chase down the long pier to the *Nedji* and into the Persian Gulf. None of it would be easy, he thought worriedly. He regarded the advancing soldiers for another second, aware of the sting of the bullet crease on his thigh, the odors of dead fires in the neighborhood and of natural gas drifting in from the oil field. A radio somewhere sounded a mournful, minor-key melody, played on a *kemancha*.

"Keep low and move fast," Durell said.

He darted into the open, Dara a step behind, her womanly figure crouched awkwardly, a frail presence in the expanse of the divided boulevard. Durell felt utterly exposed and vulnerable. He just clenched his jaw and ran as hard as he could. Dara tripped at the last moment and fell forward and struck the grassy center island with a gasp that to Durell's tense hearing sounded like a bomb exploding. On hands and knees she joined him behind a spiky planting of aloes.

They had made it halfway.

But the soldiers were moving closer.

Crickets shrilled angrily in the lovingly watered grass as Durell regarded the troops. Surf drew long, thumping sounds from the beach and harbor breakwater.

"Ready?" he whispered.

Dara nodded.

Durell took a last, quick look to read her beautiful face. Her eyes were calm and indomitable. Then he darted into what seemed to be an eternity of deadly, open space. . . .

Chapter 12

Major Ethan Rabinovitch had not slept well in his cramped, dank bunk aboard the *Nedji*. The air was hot and still in his cabin, and his sweat dampened the sheets. The odor of mildew and dead fish, or floating garbage and cockroaches filled his nose. It was not the physical discomfort that troubled him. He'd had worse beds and been glad for them.

He was reminded of the spring of 1943 and the arduous flight from Austria that he and his father had begun then. All of their relatives had disappeared, rounded up by the Nazi SS, freighted like so many cattle off to the extermination camps. Aided by friends, he and his father had hidden for months in the cellar of an abandoned and dilapidated old porcelain works, located between the Danube River and its canal just south of Vienna. But they knew time was against them and decided to run for it.

They hid like animals and they killed like animals as they passed successfully from one partisan band to the next, working their way south through Yugoslavia and then east, across Greece to neutral Turkey. Even then, they had to be smuggled into the British Mandate that was Palestine.

Ethan had been ten years old when their trek started. He was twelve, and the war was over, when they arrived in Tel Aviv.

Later, he had fought with the *Palmach* commandos of the Jewish underground against the British. At fifteen, he had been a machine gunner in the war for independence —his father had died in that conflict.

In the 1956 Sinai Campaign, Ethan had served as a combat intelligence specialist, and he went from that into the dark, unceasing danger of espionage and counter-intelligence.

Fear had been eradicated as nearly as humanly possible from the mentality of Major Ethan Rabinovitch—so it was not fear, either, that had troubled him as he lay in the dark cabin with the wind moaning outside.

He was worried about Dara.

He knew she was highly competent and fully qualified for her job. But the work of this young, fiery *Sabra* against Black September and its terrorist allies in Sweden and Paris had been nothing compared with this assignment behind Arab lines. For four years Ethan had brought her along in the business, carefully matching her tasks to her growing skills, and she had sought tougher and tougher missions each time.

But now, he did not know. . . .

Dara was almost like a daughter to the bulldoggish, bitter-eyed man.

When he had heard the distant bark of guns, he'd told himself that it was foolish and irrational to suppose that she was out there in the dark streets. She would be somewhere safely in the orbit of the Cajun, in whom he had supreme confidence. The gunfire, he told himself, was just another flare-up of the street violence that had been turning this torn and smoking capital upside down for the last twenty-four hours.

His thick, muscular legs swung off the bunk, still clad in the white sailor's gown, and he hit the switch of his radio channel scanner.

"Sir?" Chaim awakened to the scramble of static.

"It's nothing. I couldn't sleep," the major replied.

A moment passed. Then the radio spoke in Arabic: *"Resident reports subjects south of Huwaimil Souk, moving west."*

A crackling silence. Chaim sat up, hard rib-flesh rippling beneath his unbuttoned vest of gold cloth. He sounded concerned. "Do you think they are ours, sir?"

Major Rabinovitch's voice was gruff. "There's no reason to."

"It's just another disturbance." Chaim yawned as the scanner hissed and sputtered. "Care for some coffee, sir?"

The major waved him to silence as another Arabic voice spoke. But it was too late, and he missed the meaning of the transmission. He vented a growl of frustration.

Another fragment. ". . . *believed to be in the vicinity of Ghaziyah Boulevard.* . . ."

A wave of unease engulfed the major as he realized the chase had neared the old harbor, where the *Nedji* was moored. He sat on his bunk heavily, and his lips creased into a frown.

"There haven't been any more shots," Chaim said. "It could be looters, anybody. I think I'll put on the coffee."

". . . *said he saw them approach Ghaziyah Boulevard. Are the troops on station?"* The voice had an English or American accent. Major Rabinovitch knew of Pat Mc-Namara. The intelligence chief would not be involved in any ordinary chase.

He told Chaim to forget the coffee. "Break out the binoculars," he said, sounding tired and irritable. His tone might have been an attempt to cover the apprehension that touched his eyes.

He took the binoculars and climbed out of the dark cabin. The sky was milky with stars, and the breeze soughed around the mast and long lateen yard. He needed no glasses to see the troops as they spread out along the thinly lighted boulevard. The thoroughfare was on an embankment some eight feet above the pier where the *Nedji* was moored, and the soldiers stood out like a row of stakes.

Somehow the major knew that Dara was in the dark shadows beyond the boulevard. He pressed the glasses to his eyes, thumbed the focus knob, saw nothing in a scan of the black street entrances, where they opened onto the thoroughfare. He cursed the robe that bound up his legs as he crouched, yanked it loose and settled to his knees on the poop. Again he peered through the masts and bowsprits between the *Nedji* and the pale luminesence of the avenue, the glasses trembling slightly in his hands.

The scanner hissed a snatch of Arabic: ". . . *a yellow-haired foreign woman with him. . . ."*

The words came on a soft electronic breath that jolted the Israeli major with triphammer force. He had known the truth but had not wished to believe it. Now he had no choice. His face showed nothing. He kept his gaze on the boulevard and pursed his lips in thought.

Not only were Dara and the Cajun out there—they were leading the enemy to his spy ship. He judged that only the most extreme necessity had pushed them to risk revealing everything. He had to weigh that against the possible loss of the *Nedji* with her secret gear and codes. He reached a decision instantly.

Tactics now required the sacrifice of a pawn.

Major Rabinovitch bent to the ebony hole that was the hatch opening. "Chaim?" he called softly.

"Sir?"

"Hand up the Uzi."

Starlight greased the flanged sights of the submachine gun as Chaim's hand thrust the stubby weapon into the open.

"I heard the transmission, sir. I want to come with you." Chaim's voice managed to combine diffidence with the desert-thorn toughness that had seen him through a life of uncertainty and conflict.

"Denied." The major's voice was flat, his eyes still on the boulevard. He did not think he had much time. "Cast off and hold her against the pier with the diesel," he said. "Be ready to get under way immediately."

He heard the diesel crank up as he hopped to the heavy timbers of the pier and went with silent, hurried stride through the night toward the boulevard. The palace clock was an orange moon that hung over his left shoulder. It was ten after two. A rat scuttered along a mooring rope. Down under the water something twisted and showed a sickly flash of light.

The soldiers were not watching the dark pier.

Their eyes were aimed across the boulevard, toward the city, as he threw himself flat on the rough planks. He did not feel the splinters that seared the heels of his hands. Every sense was concentrated on the job that he must do when Dara and the Cajun broke cover toward him.

In two leaping strides, Durell reached the middle of the open traffic lanes, his body thrown forward and eyes fastened on the lip of the embankment that led to the *Nedji*'s pier. Dara was somewhere behind, a rush of breath and a patter of heels. The nearest soldier was about seventy-five yards down the street to Durell's left. The corner of Durell's eye caught a startled motion down there, and a shout of alert punctured the night, and then the flat, spiteful stammering of automatic rifle fire. He yanked his head into his shoulders and strained for the shelter beyond the embankment, three quick bounds away.

Bullets spanged against the pavement, shrilled through the sky, puffed, sparked, and hollowed the air in crazy ricochets.

Durell tumbled over the verge, into the shadows, and the impact of the fall crushed the breath out of him. His gut hurt so much he could not move for a second. Through the pain he was aware of Dara rolling down the incline, maybe dead, maybe alive, her ripped dress flapping and twisting around her thighs.

Durell scrambled up, kicking sand.

With a quick sense of relief, he saw Dara's hand reach up for a lift. He yanked her violently to her feet, ran to the pier and leaped onto its boards, headed for the *Nedji*. He outdistanced the slower woman, but he could not afford to wait or worry as the soldiers dashed in pursuit.

The soldiers fired wildly, on the run.

The slugs made wicked whishing sounds, like steel wires whipped against the wind.

Major Rabinovitch saw Durell thumping toward him with Dara a few yards behind and held his fire. He had watched and waited cooly as they lunged across the boulevard and down the embankment. He had lain very still and quiet in the middle of the pier as they ran along the beach and mounted the pier, the soldiers scampering after them, up on the boulevard.

The Uzi had a relatively short range. He knew he must not waste his chance.

Oddly, he did not concern himself with Dara now, or even the success of the mission, which was more important than any of them. Something else kept going through his mind, the story of Masada, a great Jewish fortress whose thousand defenders, men, women, and children, outnumbered six-to-one by the battle-hardened Roman Tenth Legion, had killed themselves rather than submit to defeat at the end of a three-year seige in 73 A.D.

Every graduate of Israel's military academy, including Major Ethan Rabinovitch, had taken an oath: "Masada shall not fall again."

The soldiers were on the pier now, far back of Dara and the Cajun. The timbers shook under the commotion, as the major pulled the cocking handle of the Uzi to the rear and squeezed the grip safety.

Then Durell's big frame loomed above, almost ran over him, jerked back.

Major Rabinovitch's voice was gruff and urgent: "Keep going. Get to the boat!"

Durell hesitated only a fraction and was gone.

Dara came next, all out of breath. "Ethan!" she cried, amid the hum of bullets.

"Keep moving!" the major bellowed with frantic insistence.

Now he was alone again, as the soldiers came on in a solid mass down the sluice of the pier. He couldn't miss if he tried, he thought grimly, and squeezed the trigger. Soldiers caught by surprise lurched, pitched, and tumbled, the ones bringing up the rear turning to run for the shore, followed by efficient, deadly bursts from the Uzi.

But the armored car had snorted to the verge of the embankment, and its turret-mounted 7.62 mm. began ripping down the pier toward the Israeli major's muzzle flashes.

Durell had reached the *Nedji* when he glanced back and saw the car's spotlight cast a ring of white brilliance around Rabinovitch. The major lurched up to a defiant bulldog stance, fired again, and screamed something.

All Durell could make out was, "Masada."

Major Ethan Rabinovitch died then in a whirlwind of lead and flying splinters.

Durell jumped aboard the *Nedji* as Dara ran out of the darkness, winded, mouth slack and trembling. She scrambled over the gunwale, and he shouted to Chaim: "Cast off!"

"The major—" Chaim began.

"The major didn't make it," Durell said. He pulled Dara's shivering body down below the shelter of the gunwale as the sleek *zarook* slid away into the blowing night. "Don't look back," he said.

She spoke in a low, tight voice. "We always look back, we Jews. It's what keeps us going, but maybe you wouldn't understand." Her long hazel eyes held a shell of tears that did not fall.

Durell knew the story of Masada, but all he said was: "Rabinovitch made his own choice."

Chaim came up. "We're out of the harbor, Mr. Durell."

He surveyed the darkness that surrounded them. "I think we sneaked out without being seen. What course do you want to set?"

"Fifty-five degrees will do. If we can catch Task Force Talon, it will pick us up—once in its vicinity, you can home in on its command frequency, it's not under radio silence. If we miss it, we should raise the coast of Iran by noon. My people will take care of us there."

"And then?" Dara questioned.

Durell's eyes turned dark and thoughtful. "And then on to Istanbul to find the Thirteenth Princess. Dhubar's oil is absolutely vital to the U.S. Without it, our economy disintegrates, and the Sixth Fleet is just so much junk."

"Have you considered that may be what she wants?"

Durell stared at Dara for a moment. Then he said: "Want it or not, she's going to clear us with Sheik Zeid— before he turns off the spigot."

Chapter 13

"Something moved down there," Dara told Durell.

"Where?"

"Second window from the left."

"Can you make it out?"

She rested her elbows on the bank of the gully, steadied the binoculars and peered down past rooftops at Princess Nadine's red-tiled *yali*. "It's gone now. It was somebody."

"Keep watching."

"How's your leg?" Dara asked from behind the glasses.

"Adequate," Durell said. He had managed to put out of his mind the wound he had suffered the night before in Dhubar, but her mention brought a dull ache to his awareness. He worked at forgetting it again, considering he had more immediate problems of survival—Dhubaran intelligence, Interpol, possibly Turkish Security.

Until he came up with the Thirteenth Princess, and lots of explanations, he was little better off than a criminal on the run.

And he needn't expect due process of law, if caught—just a bullet in the head or the crashing impact of a speeding truck.

He brushed grit from his palms and stood up, aware that the torn muscle of his left thigh had stiffened somewhat beneath the naval doctor's neat stitching. The gully was in the shade now, but he could have wished it cooler. Its torrent-smoothed stones radiated heat gathered earlier from the sun, and the sky still was hot and yellow. Flies flitted about a summer-thin trickle of water that slid soundlessly over green slime. He swung his gaze from the blue glare of the Bosporus and scrutinized a narrow street above the stone culvert behind him. He decided he was reasonably well shielded from view and looked back down the steep hill, where the wealthy hid their villas among cypresses and poplars. Nearby was the Valley of Galleys, where Mehmet the Conquerer's men had hauled their fighting ships from the Bosporus overland to the chain-blocked Golden Horn, outwitting the defenders of Constantinople in 1453. *Dolmabahce Sarayi,* the Victorian-oriental extravaganza that was the last palace of the Ottoman sultans, was down there by the water's edge now. Further up the eighteen-mile waterway that connected the Black Sea with the Sea of Marmara was the great span of the Bosporus suspension bridge. Commuters' cars, bound for Uskudar or Vanikoy on the Asian side, shared lanes with long-distance truckers from London and Teheran. In the opposite direction gleaming domes and graceful minarets brooded over old Istanbul.

"How much longer must we do this?" Dara asked.

Impatience showed through the heat flush on her freckled face.

"An hour, two hours. As long as it takes. I'd like to be sure she's alone before I go down."

"What if she owns both the Alfa and the Continental parked in her drive?"

"Just be patient. Give me the glasses. Take a break."

"Wait." The soft lines of Dara's figure hardened attentively beneath her button-belted linen skirt. She wore an open-necked white blouse and a madras plaid jacket. "Someone's coming out. It's Prince Tahir." She regarded Durell with calm expectancy.

"Let me see." Durell peered through the glasses as the prince bent his tall, thin body into the Alfa Romeo; then he straightened and handed the binoculars back to Dara. "You'll tail him," he said.

Dara pushed at the windblown straws of her short hair. "Do you think he came here because of Princess Ayla?"

"What else?"

"I suppose he hoped to comfort Nadine."

"He doesn't seem the type for comforting. Get the car turned around."

Dara made her way up the side of the gully, Durell admiring the heave of her compactly rounded hips, then disappeared beyond the stone culvert. He watched the *yali*. A Russian freighter with a winged star at the point of its bow churned sluggishly by. The Bosporus was busy with white-hulled ferries, pleasure craft, and brilliantly painted caïques. There was a dim murmur of diesels and plash of bow waves against the background street noises of Istanbul's sprawling suburbs.

The Alfa charged up the hill, disappeared from view, then whipped over the culvert, and a clash of gears told Durell that Dara had cut in behind it with the rental Mercedes.

Nadine's *yali* was a wooden house in the old Ottoman style—oriental gingerbread, Moorish arches within arches, and delicate, flowerlike latticework between supports of a veranda that overhung the spangled water.

The platinum-haired woman answered the doorbell herself—no servants were in evidence, and Durell guessed

there hadn't been time to employ any since her arrival
from London.

She took one look at him with her wide blue eyes and
told him to get lost.

"Just a moment." Durell leaned against the heavy
door. "I'm wanted for kidnaping, thanks to your
daughter."

"Don't tell me your troubles, after the mess you made
of things."

She made a move to close the steel-studded door, but
Durell shoved through, holding his temper. His voice was
low and grinding. "Tell me where she is, Nadine."

"Get out of here." The deep cleavage of her breasts
heaved angrily around a diamond-pendant—she wore an
off-the-shoulder blouse of hot pink color and a long,
pleated white skirt.

Durell looked beyond her and saw the Bosporus
through the glass wall of a sitting room. There was an
enormous dome-shaped fireplace, red tulips in a blue-
glazed Turkish pot, wall hangings of Bursa and Gordes
carpets, and mirrors. Lots of mirrors. "Is Princess Ayla
here? I can search the house."

"You must have scared her out of her wits."

"I'm the one who's scared." Durell held her shoulders.
They felt small and crushable in his grip. He controlled
himself.

"You've never been scared a day in your life, Sam
Durell. You don't know what it means. I told you, buzz
off."

"You haven't answered my question."

"What?"

"Is she here?"

"No." Nadine shrugged away from his grasp.

"Where is she, then?"

"I don't know." She saw the darkening look in his
eyes and faltered. Then, defiantly, "All right, I'm not
saying, like it or lump it." A bit of Alabama had crept
into her pronunciation.

"Now we're making progress," Durell said.

"Wrong, buster. It's a dead end for you. I didn't tell
Tahir anything, and I'm not telling you."

Durell saw that she was angry because she was genuinely frightened. It wasn't an act. He did not know if she was afraid of him or Tahir or something else. He spoke more gently. "At least you admit you've seen her."

"What if I have?"

"She may be in danger. I want to help."

"Not out of the goodness of your heart, you don't. You've got your own reasons."

"It comes to the same thing."

"Tell it to Sheik Zeid. I'm going to let him handle everything this time. I shouldn't have gone behind his back before."

"He's in Istanbul?"

"He will be this evening. I called him."

Alarm sharpened Durell's tone. "You'll get him killed, you little idiot."

"He can take care of himself—and his wife."

"Where will he be staying?"

"Why do you want to know?"

"You directed me to him."

Nadine studied his face with lifted gaze, as if suspecting him of some kind of trickery, but then she said: "The Buyuk Tarabya."

"Thanks."

"Just go ahead and go there if you want to see what color your guts are."

Durell let that slide off, wrote the number of his own hotel on a slip of paper, and handed it to her. "You're going to need more help than you think before this is over," he said. "You can reach me there."

Nadine opened the door. "You've done nothing but let me down," she ranted. "First with Volkan, and now with Ayla."

Durell stepped out gingerly, favoring his weak leg, and turned to face her in the warm, deepening shade of the house. "Things haven't gone exactly as any of us planned," he said.

"Go suck an egg."

The door slammed in his face.

He walked to the Kabatas ferry landing, cursing the prickly heat and his leg and Nadine as he went. She was in a position to save him lots of trouble, if she ever came to her senses.

No one seemed to have followed him from her *yali*, but he took a *dolmus* rather than a conventional taxi as an added precaution. *Dolmus* means "stuffed" in Turkish, and that exactly described the jam-packed car that stopped every block or so to pick up or let off passengers. It reeked of stale tobacco and sour milk, perhaps because the Turks loved yoghurt so, and he traded its crowded anonymity for a taxi at Tophane Fountain.

The last rays of the sun burned in wispy clouds, and evening sat on Istanbul soft and warm, like a brilliant bird on a jeweled egg, as he crossed the Golden Horn below the domes of St. Sophia and the Sultan Ahmet Mosque, their minarets ringed with lights. Busy Galata Bridge seemed a world unto itself. Big white ferries were lined up two abreast at landings on the lower level, where there were ticket offices, kiosks selling lemonade and cheese-and-tomato rolls, and newsstands. He came off the bridge at Emino Square, passed men washing their feet in a fountain by the wall of the four-hundred-year-old New Mosque—which had a lighted sign strung between its minarets—and wound up the seven-hilled city through a jumble of wooden tenements and gloomy caravanserais. The streets were packed. Porters bent double under incredible loads shuffled between the trolley buses to mingle on the sidewalks with white-suited sherbet-water sellers, hand-holding soldiers, students with smoldering eyes, and countless tourists.

Durell left the taxi at a side street, near Alemdar Caddesi where buses ran up to Sultan Ahmet Mosque, surveyed the traffic with a quick eye, pressed liras into the driver's hand. He strolled past the grassy expanse of the Roman Hippodrome, with its obelisk from the temple of Karnak and Serpentine Column from the temple of Delphi.

He hoped he would not have to lean on Nadine, but the stakes always were so enormous in his line of work that it would not be a first of its kind if he did.

There were no limits. There was only one prohibition: "Thou shalt leave no tracks."

His hotel was not far from Sirkeci Station, eastern terminus of the Orient Express. It was named the Palace Oteli after nearby Topkapi Palace, which it resembled as a rat hole resembles Carlsbad Caverns. Shabby shops and cheap restaurants that smelled tantalizingly of roasting kebabs and grilling *köfte* stretched away on either side of the hotel's portals, which were plastered with posters for movies, cabarets, and old elections. He had chosen the place with deliberate care to avoid as long as possible the agents of Pat McNamara. He knew they would be coming. It was only a matter of time.

The front desk was in a wooden cage that showed dents and bald turnings where the varnish had worn away, the lobby narrow and dimly lighted. His room, reached by two flights of tired stairs that did his bad leg no favors, had the benefit of a window that looked onto a cool garden cinema. A spaghetti western was on the bill for tonight. Beyond was a glimpse of purple water, the dusky wrinkle of Asian hills.

He draped the jacket of his new blue suit over a chair, drank two tumblers of tap water, and lay down for a rest.

It did not last more than a few minutes.

The phone rang, and it was Dara, and she said she was being followed.

Chapter 14

"Where are you?" Durell asked Dara.

"In the lobby."

"You shouldn't have come here. You should have ditched him first."

"Don't you want a look at him? I couldn't take him all by myself."

"Who wants him?"

"I do, Sam. Badly. For debts owed—like Ethan."

Durell's voice was harsh. "Then go collect. Meanwhile, I'll have to move us out of this place. You've blown it."

"Sam—? Please?"

He hesitated, sucked in a calming breath. "What does he look like?"

"I couldn't tell. He's parked down the block in a blue Renault."

Durell said nothing for a moment. He shared her feelings but would have saved his luck for the big ones—you threw back the small fry because they could be deadly but, often as not, unrewarding.

"The damage is done, Sam," Dara said. "You might as well help me."

"Walk up to the *Kapaliçarsi,* the Great Bazaar—you know where it is?"

"I came by it."

"Not the Spice Bazaar, down by the Horn."

"I know."

"Remember my bum leg. Take it slow."

"Sam? Thanks."

"There's always the chance it will be worthwhile," he said, and hung up.

When he got outside, he saw that she had passed the Renault and that a hulking figure was crawling out of it to follow her. Night had fallen now, and the poor lighting made him little more than a silhouette as he ambled casually behind her. Durell kept up with little effort, one eye on the springy shine of Dara's yellow hair so as not to lose her in the distance, the other on the big man.

He caught a hungry whiff of hot pastries and coffee as he passed a *pastahane* cafe.

He refused the entreaties of a shoeshine boy.

He followed, and nothing happened.

Then Dara stopped, and he saw the pale shine of her

face as she looked back. The big man stopped and looked in a shop window. Durell turned back to the shoeshine boy, raised a shoe to the footrest. When the others moved on, he tipped the bewildered youngster for a half-polished shoe and fell in behind.

The Great Bazaar, despite its imposing name, loomed into view as an insignificant cluster of roofs and dingy streets. It was a Byzantine structure, once probably the royal carriage stables, and had no apparent entrance, since most of its arched doorways lay down back streets. Its enormous roof sheltered a maze of streets and alleys, and almost anything could be found in there for a price. Durell knew of a Kurdish chieftain who had consummated a major arms purchase there.

Dara went inside on the Street of Gold, where the dusty air was hazed yellow by reflections of glittering display windows. The way was thronged with shoppers, hawkers, black market operators, tourists, pimps, and purse snatchers. Bargaining was carried on with a loud *"Yok!* No!" and a violent shrug of the shoulders. Young men just back from the factories of Germany studied with earnest eyes golden discs they would buy for their betrothed ones. Music blared.

Dara sat at a table in an open-fronted coffee shop. Durell joined her, looked left and right.

"Over there," she said.

He followed her gaze.

The huge man lounged before a display of golden baubles. The man's thumb smoothed the enormous crescents of his mustache as he smiled, nodded—and came toward them.

"Oh, hell," Durell muttered. "It's Volkan again."

"Ah, Durell Bey. And his lovely lady."

"Care to join us?" Durell said. He pushed out a chair.

Volkan chortled, his bald head gleaming. *"Tesekkür ederim*—thanks." He rubbed Durell's shoulder with the Turkish love for touching and sat down with a windy sigh. "This is good. Yes, it is good we can be civilized."

"Not too civilized." Durell smiled grimly. "I have a .45 aimed at your gut under the table."

Volkan's grin froze. Sweat popped from his head, reminding Durell of a squeezed sponge.

"Why did you follow the lovely lady?" Durell asked.

"To find you, of course. What would I want with her? Women are good only for the kitchen and the bed. Agreed?"

Durell suppressed a grin. Dara shot him a stinging glance. Durell said: "It seems I found you first. It may cost you dearly."

"Put the gun away. Please."

"Just don't think about it. Where did you pick up Dara's tail?"

"At the dock."

Dara said: "Prince Tahir boarded a big cabin cruiser. That was where I lost him."

"He went to his house in the Prince's Islands, not far from here," Volkan said.

Durell spoke. "Princess Nadine called you a spy."

"Ah. Another woman, you understand. Too excitable for my taste."

"Was she right?"

"Do you have Princess Ayla?" Volkan was evading the question.

"Of course not."

A waiter brought them strong black coffee in small floral cups. Its fragrance was delicious. The vast hubbub in the Street of Gold made a sound like a waterfall

"This affair can be ended by the return of Princess Ayla," Volkan said. He sipped with a noise of polite relish.

"I think not," Durell said. "It has to run its course, like a bad sickness, a lethal illness. Too much happened in Dhubar for it to stop so simply. Events have been set in motion for some purpose."

"Possibly. It is not our business. We don't want Dhubar's troubles brought here."

Durell stared at him for a moment. "Who is 'we'?"

The man's big paw held out a leather identification case. "Turkish Security," he said.

"Don't look so surprised," Volkan said. "I was planted in Prince Tahir's entourage long ago. It pays to keep track of royalty, especially when it has pretensions to the throne of your country."

The ID looked authentic to Durell. He shoved his Marine .45, requisitioned on a carrier the night before, back into his waistband, and exchanged glances with Dara, who carried his gun's twin in her shoulder bag.

A disappointed blush burned on her cheeks. "Let's go, Sam."

"It isn't that simple, is it, Volkan?" Durell said.

"I have been instructed to work with you," Volkan replied.

"Meaning we have no choice?"

"The alternative is arrest and deportation."

Dara stood up. "Let them try to catch us, Sam. I don't trust this man."

Durell told her to sit down. "Let's give him a chance."

"I will be a valuable ally." Volkan smiled, and the tips of his mustache almost touched his nose.

Durell turned to Dara. "Where did Prince Tahir go after leaving Nadine's?"

"Should we discuss business here?" Volkan said.

"Why not? No one's close enough to overhear. It can't be bugged."

Dara said: "He went straight to the boat, except for a stop at No. 50 Black Stone Street near the Sultan Ahmet Mosque. It looked like a private residence, a walled villa—except for one thing."

"What was that?"

Dara swung her eyes to Volkan, then back to Durell. "It had guards at the gate," she said. "They looked like regular Turkish infantry."

"Who lives there?" Durell asked Volkan.

The big Turk narrowed his eyes, pushed his chin with a forefinger. "That is the house of General Nezih Abdurrahman—a fine soldier. A patriot."

"Save the endorsements. What's his command?"

Volkan hesitated. His eyes showed reluctance. *"Özür dilerim*—I'm sorry—that may be classified."

"Then declassify it, if you are our ally." Durell's hand found the grip of his pistol.

"Wait. Just a minute. You see, I am not at liberty—"

Dara's voice was a low threat as she told Durell: "Let's take this hulk into the alley and dispose of him."

"Well, perhaps I can release the information." Volkan swallowed, his thick throat quivering. "After all, what's the harm, eh?" He shrugged. "He commands an armored division."

"A combat division." Durell's voice tightened. "Would it be stationed on Cyprus, by any chance?"

"As a matter of fact, it is, although normally posted in Cappadocia, in central Turkey."

"Sam!" Dara's voice lifted with excitement. "Didn't McNamara tell you that the old emir's assassin was traced as far as Cyprus?"

Durell stared at her, then at Volkan. Their table was an island of momentary silence in the roar of the bazaar. Then Durell told the other two to wait while he made a phone call. As he left, he saw Dara's hand slip into her purse, doubtlessly to rest on her gun. She still did not trust Volkan, and he thought that was just as well.

Neither did he.

He bought a token, dropped it into the slot of a public telephone, spoke a couple of minutes, and returned to the table. "General Abdurrahman's division is scheduled for routine rotation back to the mainland in a day or two," he told Dara.

She saw the look on his face and said: "Is that bad?"

"Only if the division commandeers its transports for a landing in Dhubar instead." His blue eyes were dark and grave.

"I'd give anything to know what Prince Tahir and the general talked about," she said.

Durell spoke thoughtfully. "When people are at the hub of history in the making, they sometimes keep records. Journals, correspondence. . . ."

"What are you thinking?" Volkan asked, his face wary.
"Let's break into your general's study," Durell said.
"Maybe we'll find out just what kind of patriot he is."

Chapter 15

"We can take the guards," Dara said. "What's the problem, Sam?"

"We don't want trouble with the locals. If we fumble, the police will be on our backs." The motor of the Mercedes purred in neutral. He had parked around the corner of a park that was across the street from General Abdurrahman's house. A car passed, headed the other way, and he and Dara and Volkan sat stiffly, their faces turned, as its headlamps washed them briefly with light.

"The police will be around asking us our business, if we sit here much longer," Dara said.

"We wouldn't have a very good answer," Volkan muttered.

Durell thought a moment longer and said: "Dara. You get out with me."

"What about me?" Volkan asked.

"You will pick us up. I don't know how long this will take. Half an hour or so, not much more." Durell stepped out quietly. The light airs felt good where his back had been smothered by the car seat. Dara smoothed her dress and stood beside him as he bent to the window. "Cruise the neighborhood," he told Volkan. "Don't attract any attention."

"You're making a mistake, not letting me come with you," the big man growled unhappily.

"We'll do it this way." Durell's eyes scanned the intersection behind the car.

"What good will the woman be?" Volkan demanded.

"She may be better than you think." Durell moved toward the corner, Dara at his side. The light breeze made a yellow spray of her short hair. The Mercedes started away with an angry rip of its tires, and Dara said: "Volkan could bring the authorities down on us. Have you thought of that?"

Durell sounded calm. "I have," he said.

"I'd rather have him with us, where we can watch him."

"And he could alert the household?" Durell blew through his nose. "If I can get a look at the general's papers, I'll worry about getting away later."

Dara stopped in the shadows and raised her eyes to him. "You don't trust him, either?"

"Of course not."

"Then why bring him along?"

"To see what he does. Look, his credentials are in order. If General Abdurrahman is willing to betray his government to help Prince Tahir, there's no telling how deep the conspiracy may go."

"You mean Turkish Security . . . ?"

"Possibly." Durell's gaze darkened. "I have a feeling Volkan is trying to be clever. He will overplay his hand, if he's against us."

"But—what if he double-crosses us here—tonight?"

Durell smiled faintly. "Then we run like squirrels."

They had rounded the corner of the bushy park and walked past the two sentries, who were across the street and paid them scant attention. Below them the Golden Horn shrank to the north, where it became the Lycus River among hills that heaved away into Thrace. Lights sparkled distantly out there, embers in the ashes of night. The general's house was on spacious, well-shrubbed grounds far up the south side of the Horn, beyond the walls of Theodosius and the new beltway that connected London Highway with the Bosporus Bridge. The banks of the fabled waterway had dazzled the viewer with palaces, pleasure kiosks, and imperial gardens a century before, but now the Horn was lined with shipyards and factories for the most part. Abdurrahman lived in one of the few sedately aristocratic neighborhoods that remained. There was a plastered stone wall around his grounds, and it probably had electronic surveillance devices on it, Durell decided. Upper lights of the house glowered out of a nest of gnarled old pine trees that bent slightly in the cool breeze.

Durell had filled Dara in on the rest of his plan by the time they came to a coffeehouse at the corner of the overgrown park. Inside, men sat in a haze of smoke and played cards and backgammon or discussed politics, business, soccer as they sipped endlessly at Turkish coffee or sweet, amber tea. Some passed around the mouthpiece of a bubbling *nargile*. They stared frankly and without hostility at Durell and especially Dara. Durell remembered that tradition normally closed the doors of coffeehouses to women.

He asked the proprietor where the telephone was— *"Telefon nerededir?"*—and got a nod toward a niche in the back of the room.

He dialed and told the operator to send an ambulance to No. 50 Black Stone Street.

"General Nezih Abdurrahman," he said, "is dying of a heart attack."

They said nothing as they waited tensely just inside the dark fringe of the park. About five minutes passed, then the low clamor of the ancient city was split by an approaching siren. When the ambulance pulled up at the sentry box, Dara started to move.

"Not yet," Durell said, the back of his hand against her shoulder.

The noise drew men from the coffeehouse, and they hurried over to listen and advise in an argument that raged between the sentries and ambulance personnel.

Voices rose.

The crowd grew.

"Now," Durell said.

They stole from the foliage and crossed the street

about thirty yards from the commotion, moving casually but efficiently. The guards did not notice them. The wall was not high. They slipped along it in the shadows until they were well away from the street, then pulled themselves over easily, and their feet crunched against a matting of needles and leaves in the compound.

They did not move for a long second.

Dara stood close to Durell, her fragrance that of another flower amid the carefully cultivated beds. His breathing was light and easy, his urgency controlled as a clock spring. He felt good, but told himself to be cautious of his leg. The heckling of the bystanders came from the direction of the sentry box, and Durell twisted his face that way. Through a low filament of mingled boughs, he saw a sentry with a phone in his hand, evidently calling the house to determine whether an ambulance had been called for.

He waved Dara on after him.

There had been no alarm on crossing the wall, but the signal didn't have to be audible. Amber lights could be flashing silently all over the house.

The voices faded as the ambulance left, and Durell twisted through laurel bushes to touch a velvet of moss that grew on the stone wall of Abdurrahman's home. He saw that it was two stories high, with a main section and short wing. Frogs chirped. Pigeons bubbled and brushed under the eaves.

The darkness here was like a weight on his eyes.

He glanced up and saw the sky, just scraps and slices of a softer darkness.

He reached high, tried a window, found it locked, moved on. His soles grated against the flagstones of a terrace; French doors mirrored the night on his right. Durell worked furiously with penlight and lockpicks, felt the doors give under his push.

"Stay here," he whispered. "I'll be back in a minute."

By the low glow of his penflash he moved soundlessly around divan, table, and chairs. The air was still and smelled warmly of heavy fabrics. There was a large desk, somewhat cluttered with bric-a-brac, and fine antique weapons glinted on the walls. It could be a study, he thought gratefully. He located a closet, then thumbed off his penflash and opened the window drapes.

Back outside, he told Dara: "It's time for you to go. As a decoy you must make sure the guards see you."

She nodded, her face a pale shadow. "I understand."

There was a pause. "Don't be frightened," Durell said.

"Would it matter if I said I was?"

"No."

Her lips touched his, quickly and firmly, muffling an inarticulate syllable inside her mouth.

"Run," he said. And she was gone.

Hurriedly he turned on a table lamp and ducked into the closet, leaving the door cracked so that he could see the desk and most of one wall.

Shouts came from outdoors, the snap of a single rifle shot, tiny in here. Durell's jaw muscles stood out in ridges; sweat funneled down his neck and chest. The closet was hot and airless. He did not know if Dara had made it, wouldn't know until he got out himself—if he were so lucky.

Only one shot. Maybe they were reluctant to fire in this residential neighborhood.

Or maybe one shot was all it had taken.

Volkan had been an agent of Turkish Security for seventeen years, and this was only the second crisis he had confronted.

A man should know what to do, he thought, and slapped the wheel of the Mercedes with his big hand. His grandfather, who had been a sergeant in Mustafa Kemal Pasha's republican army, would say: "But first, a man must know who he is."

Volkan's face saddened as he peered through the windshield and the lights and shadows flickered past.

He wished he were with his grandfather, that venerated old warrior. He and most of the clan that remained in and around the small banana- and orange-growing village a mile from the Mediterranean would be camped in the Taurus Mountains at the family *yayla,* their summer retreat, in their tents of goatskin, hunting and telling the

ancient stories around the campfires, the women milking
ewes and fetching firewood and water.

Volkan no longer could bring himself to attend the
yayla.

Even on the rare occasions that Prince Tahir chose to
free him from his duties, he felt he had no right to be
there with his honorable grandfather.

Volkan had felt for a long time that he was a traitor.

Long ago, Prince Tahir had confronted him with ir-
refutable evidence, photographs that showed the hulking
bodyguard's weakness for pretty young men.

That had been the other crisis: the decision he must
make, either to report the matter to his superiors and
take the ruinous consequences, or to allow Prince Tahir
to turn him against his agency and his country. He had
chosen the latter—as Prince Tahir had known he would
—but he had never forgiven himself. It was a shame that
he had always to live with. Perhaps it had been made
easier by the grand increase in salary that Prince Tahir
had bestowed on him—over the years he had accumulated immense wealth for the son of a back-country
Turk, over $100,000 in a Swiss bank account.

But the money had not left his mind at rest.

There were always the false reports to his superiors to
remind him. His agency's file on Prince Tahir must be
three-fourths the work of Volkan's imagination by now.
Turkish Security really knew nothing about Prince Tahir
or what he did.

Volkan knew very little himself.

Having sold out, he no longer made any attempt to
find the hidden motives and meanings behind the prince's
activities, even though he was aware that the Turkish
Republic must consider such a man a potential enemy
by the nature of his birth.

Volkan had contented himself with being just what he
seemed—a bodyguard. But he had striven, in a quest for
pride of some kind, to be the best bodyguard he could be.

Now he faced another crisis, a crisis this time of even
greater magnitude. It had started simply enough. He had
followed the woman from the landing expecting that she
would lead him to Durell, had courted the hope that he

could insinuate himself into the confidence of the both of them. Prince Tahir, who seemed to have ways of finding out anything, had learned in Dhubar that the girl was with Israeli intelligence and the man an operative of America's K Section.

Volkan had acted on an axiom of the business.

The axiom said it was more decisive in the long run to learn your enemy's plans than to win a battle.

Volkan paused abruptly and wondered if Durell had operated on the same principle in taking him in so easily. But then other thoughts surged back in, drowning the moment of doubt in his tense mind.

He had hoped to discover Durell's battle plan, his allies and the threads of their linkages, his strengths and weaknesses. So he had gone along with him.

But now, he did not know. . . .

He was confused.

Why had Prince Tahir gone to General Abdurrahman? The question nettled and itched, and Volkan blew an angry breath as if to clear his frustrated mental processes. In a way he wanted to go back and help Durell now, but he feared Prince Tahir too much. And the general. What if they were caught? Worse—and here was a real thought—what if Durell had planned it so that he, Volkan, would take the whole blame?

The American was tricky.

He could just see himself trying to explain the break-in, while Durrell was out of it, running free.

Oh, no—Volkan shook his head—he wasn't going back there. It had been a mistake to come to these people on his own initiative, but it wasn't too late to correct it. He glanced at his wristwatch, decided he had waited too long to alert the general. If Durell had come and gone, there would be questions as to why he had allowed the burglary in the first place.

Volkan had another idea—he would get some of his colleagues, and Durell and his woman would be in for a nasty surprise when they returned to their hotel.

The silence that came to Durell through the crack in the closet door seemed long and ominous. He breathed shallowly and knuckled sweat from his eyesockets. The closet smelled of woolen coats and musty old files, and he detected a thin, rank odor from his own body and wished for a bath.

Less than a minute had passed when he became aware of a jarring of floorboards as feet padded toward the room. He heard the study door open, but it was out of his view, and he did not know who came through it.

Someone spoke roughly, in Turkish: "She was in here. Look, the doors to the terrace are still open."

Another voice, young and deferential, perhaps that of an aide, said: "The room does not appear disturbed, General *effendi*. Perhaps nothing was taken."

Durell got a scent of a perfumed Hisar cigarette as quick feet moved across the heirloom Kayseri carpet, and a short, barrel-chested man came into view. His close-cropped hair was the color of gun metal, his face square and taut with instant authority. He wore a dark smoking jacket and civilian slacks, but he had to be General Abdurrahman, Durell decided. The general strode toward the open French doors, stared into the dark compound, and he told the other: "Go check with the guards. See if they ran the wench down."

Durell heard the feet of the aide as he moved off in double-time. He breathed a sigh of sweaty relief: the shot must have missed her.

General Abdurrahman snapped the French doors shut and surveyed the room, hands on hips, leathery face intent.

"Huh. A woman," he snorted.

Then he stepped impatiently to the wall behind the desk, reached to a painting of caïques working the Bosporus against a background of Topkapi Saray's cliff-like walls, pressed a corner of its antique frame. A spring-loaded panel to which the frame was attached swung out and revealed a wall safe.

A slow second of dread passed through Durell as the general glanced over his shoulder, seeming to glare straight at the narrow slit in the closet door. Then Abdurrahman turned back to the safe.

Durell could not see the numbers on the dial, but he memorized the direction of turn: a free spin, then left, right, right, left. A yank at the chrome handle, and the general thrust his hand inside, withdrew a brown paper envelope, and turned it in his hands, seeming to relax suddenly. He did not trouble to open it but replaced it swiftly and snapped the wall panel back into place.

With a last look around the room, he switched off the lamp and left.

So far everything had gone just as Durell had hoped—it had been reasonable to expect the general to go straight to that which he most feared to lose and make sure that it had not been taken.

Durell had no idea what the brown envelope contained, but he judged the gamble would have been worth the trouble if he could get it. He counted to ten, touched open the closet door, crept across the hush of the soft Kayseri carpet. With a thought for the armed soldiers somewhere just outside, he shielded his penflash as best he could and went to work.

There were countless makes of locks, but he knew they could be narrowed to a few types that shared many similarities. In IPE—for Illegal, Perilous Entry—he had been taught at the Farm the refinements on everything from door locks and padlocks to safes and bank vaults. And how to outwit them with simple tools and cunning touch.

The general's safe was good.

But it was old and rather noisy.

A tumbler fell. Durell took his time. Reverse—another tumbler. Half a minute went by. He gave the handle an easy pull, and the round door glided open on oiled hinges.

A leather jewel case blunted the beam of his penflash, then a small strongbox.

The brown envelope lay on top of the strongbox. Red wax sealed its flap, and stamped into it was the curving image of a scimitar. Durell's pulse quickened a beat as he recognized the national emblem of Dhubar.

Aware that the envelope could have been delivered

here by Prince Tahir and that its contents would be of the utmost gravity, he closed both safe and wall panel with trembling fingers.

He moved outdoors, hustled from shadow to shadow as best as his sore leg would allow. A fresh scent of mowed grass came across the lawn. Two sentries stood by the floodlighted drive entrance, but they did not appear to be the ones seen earlier, and he swallowed a surge of apprehension as it dawned on him that there must be a guard barracks in the compound.

The wall came up through the blurring shadows, and he heaved himself over, holding his heart down in his chest, eyes on the sentries.

A guard turned abruptly toward the gatehouse.

The silent sentry console must be in there, Durell thought—and this time the guards were not distracted. One of the men sprinted toward the place where he had crossed over, while the other, his back turned to Durell, grabbed excitedly for the telephone.

With the wall still blinding the first sentry to him, Durell saw his chance to cross the street into the park and took it.

He forgot his complaining leg and ran like a squirrel.

Chapter 16

"Dara?" Durell whispered.

"Dara?" he repeated, and glanced back through the park shrubbery at the general's house.

"Sam?" She came through flowering bushes and unkempt grass, a ripple of shadow on his left. "Any luck?"

He saw the .45 in her hand. "Some," he said. "Are you all right?"

"It was a near thing. I lost them below Feshane Caddesi."

"They probably were called off when the general decided nothing had been taken." Durell saw that the pair of sentries had been joined by two more soldiers and an officer. A jabbering discussion was going on, and the gist of it seemed based on the officer's contention that the second alarm must have been a malfunction. It was clear that Durell had not been seen as he slipped away. He breathed a bit easier.

"I was surprised that they didn't call the police," Dara said.

"The general must want to keep the authorities out of this." He walked across the park until he was sure that they were out of sight to the sentries and sat down behind some bushes. "Seen Volkan?" he asked as he took the envelope from inside his jacket.

"What do you think?"

"I don't know—he didn't alert General Abdurrahman."

"I think he was too clever. You finessed him." She looked like a child, sitting on her knees, the pale shine of her teeth showing in a smile. "What have you got there?" she asked as Durell broke the seal on the envelope.

He held his flash to the document that was unfolded, saw that it was typed in Arabic on rich, heavy paper and bore the signature of Sheik Zeid. Immediately below that was the seal of state.

She put her cheek next to his and read along with him, then drew in a breath and spoke in a low, grating voice that sometimes came to her in moments of alarm. "This makes Princess Ayla regent of Dhubar if anything happens to Sheik Zeid."

Durell nodded. "Meaning she runs the country until her son comes of age."

"And Prince Tahir would be the power behind the throne!" She sank down. "Oh, Sam—I have a feeling he won't be satisfied with just Dhubar."

"Don't panic. Sheik Zeid isn't dead yet," Durell said.

"This shatters Moslem tradition, you know—women just don't reign in those countries." Her voice turned hopeful. "Perhaps it can't be enforced."

"Traditions have been broken before." Durell paused. "As for enforcement—think about where we found this."

"General Abdurrahman's armored division! But surely Sheik Zeid wouldn't be a party to Turkish intervention."

Durell spoke warningly. "Prince Tahir would."

"Sheik Zeid must have been out of his mind to sign that."

Durell's voice turned thoughtful. "He may have feared that if he died, the people would reject his son because of his Ottoman blood. In that light it was prudent to name a regent who was certain to be sympathetic to the crown prince. He must not know that the document is in General Abdurrahman's possession."

"Wouldn't the general require the backing of his government for an expedition to Dhubar?"

"He might try it solo. If he were successful, he'd probably be a national hero, and the government's hands would be tied. The Turks haven't forgotten their glory days, when they ran things from Athens right around the Mediterranean to North Africa."

"And all Sheik Zeid intended was to make his wife regent if he died sometime in the vague future, if there were an illness or an accident—"

"Right," Durell broke in. "And that accident could happen tomorrow—or tonight—or at any moment." He added grimly, "But it won't be an accident. They plan to kill him."

He got to his feet, and Dara rose beside him, straight and lovely. "What are you going to do now?" she asked.

"Put you in a taxi for our safe house—I don't trust the hotel. Then confront Sheik Zeid with this. He's in Istanbul."

"But he's after your head."

"I have to try to make him see the light," Durrell said.

"If the Turks go in, the Arabs won't tolerate it. The Mideast will go up in flames, with Israel right in the middle of the bonfire." She took a short breath. "Sheik Zeid had better renounce that document, or. . . ."

"Or what?"

Dara's eyes narrowed. "Or I'll find Princess Ayla—by myself, if necessary—and she won't live to be regent."

It was almost ten o'clock when they parted, intending to meet later at K Section's safe house in the *gecekondu,* workers' slum, further up the Horn. The night was cool, the city quieting down even in the consulate section that was focused on Taksim Square and Istiklal Caddesi, Istanbul's narrow, pulsing equivalent of Fifth Avenue. Down on the Bosporus searchlights played back and forth as ferries threaded among smaller craft.

Durell left his taxi just before Galatasaray Square, in front of a small open-air market, and turned into a narrow passageway at No. 172. It reeked of fish restaurants. He walked deliberately, testing the air, holding back a sense of urgency that threaded through his pulse.

These cramped spaces, now called *Çiçek Pasaji,* "Flower Passage," once comprised the inner court and arcades of the old Pera City Hall, seat of the European community in Constantinople. They were crowded with beer halls and restaurants, and people, mostly men as usual, walked about munching *kokerec,* grilled lamb's intestines. From a basement beer hall came an oriental drinking song, and Durell heard the wail and beat of a strolling duo on clarinet and drum.

He paused, saw no evidence that he had caught anyone's attention, moved on through the ebb and flow of the crowd, and passed out of the walls by way of the empty flower market where blossoms crushed on the stones perfumed the stale air.

So far so good, he thought.

He wished he knew where Volkan was.

He did not know who had knowledge of Sheik Zeid's presence in town. He suspected it was a well-kept secret, but there was a chance that his hotel was staked out.

He decided to take a bath.

The sign for a *hammam* was just down the street. He went inside and exchanged his shoes for a pair of rubber slippers, wrote a message on the back of the envelope with the broken seal, and gave the hovering shoeshine boy a fifty-lira note to deliver it to Sheik Zeid.

He felt reasonably confident that Zeid would come.

Then an attendant showed him to his cubicle. Someone snored beyond the partition, and he recalled that a steamed and scrubbed Turk usually returned to his cubicle for tea and a nap before going out to face the world again. It seemed a civilized tradition, he thought as he undressed and wrapped a towel about his waist. He peeked under the bandage, blew through tightened lips, and decided to leave the wound covered. He'd have to wash around it. He had never heard of a case of thievery in a Turkish bath. The ancient institution was too highly prized and zealously guarded to allow for that. Still, he took no chances and rolled the document into a towel that he carried with him as he went back down to the main floor and into the baths. He got accustomed to the heat in the first room, then moved on to the hottest chamber and lay down on one of the wooden pallets scattered about a marble platform. The marble glistened under the wet heat that opened his pores like floodgates. Aches and pains oozed out of his awareness. As his taut body relaxed, he realized how very tired he was— but he dared not sleep.

An attendant came by, suggested a massage. Durell declined. The *hammam* was almost deserted this time of night, although there would be a surge of business after the clubs closed and the parties ended. It was quiet, except for the trickle of water, the dim clank of a copper bowl, or occasional shuffle of feet.

His call from the bazaar earlier had gone to Rob Thawley, an intelligence officer at the U.S. Consulate, and Thawley had reported that General Abdurrahman's division was scheduled for rotation back to the mainland. Durell had asked for National Reconnaissance Office satellite coverage to spot the division when it sailed. The sailing might warn that all hell was about to break loose. That would be confirmed if the transports turned south for Dhubar.

Durell worried and fretted about Sheik Zeid and

Princess Ayla, and sweat crawled down his cheeks and ribs, tickling.

Condensation dripped from the domed ceiling.

The brutish smell of steam became cloying.

He rose from the pallet, entered the washing room, was scrubbed down by an attendant using a coarse cloth mitten.

"*Çok pis! Çok pis!* Very filthy! Very filthy!" said the attendant.

"Just leave the leg that way," Durell said.

The attendant doused Durell in warm water, swashed him with a horsetail pulled out of a bucket of suds, then gave him a final rinse with gallons of cooler water. "Is done," he said. "Is fine?"

"Is fine," Durell replied, and turned for the door where, a moment before, another attendant had waited to swath him against a chill with fresh towels.

But the attendant wasn't there.

Sheik Zeid was.

Pat McNamara stood behind and slightly to one side of him, showing his chopped .45 as if it were a full house, aces over. "Looks like we caught you with your pants down, old man," he said. He smiled, then frowned.

Durell made no reply but turned his gaze on the intense eyes of the emir. "Your Highness," he said politely.

"Mr. Durell." Sheik Zeid did not move. Even in a short-sleeved shirt and slacks he had a regal manner.

McNamara said: "Get your clothes on, Cajun. You're going to Dhubar."

Durell spoke as if McNamara weren't there. "Your Highness, I have something to show you. It may change the way you see things." He bent for the rolled towel.

"Touch that, and I'll blow you away," McNamara growled.

"Then you get it," Durell said.

"All I'm getting is a chill, standing in this door," McNamara said. His voice roughened. "I said get dressed. Get your ass moving."

Durell looked at the emir again. The man clearly was

troubled and becoming annoyed with McNamara into the bargain. Sheik Zeid spoke barely above a whisper. "Bring the towel to me."

Durell complied, and the little emir unrolled the towel and found the folded document. He recognized the paper as he must have the envelope and glanced at Durell as he straightened it. When he saw what was written on it, he spoke with deadly calm: "Where did you obtain this?"

"From the house of General Nezih Abdurrahman, here in Istanbul."

Zeid turned to McNamara. "Do we know this Abdurrahman?"

McNamara's sloped shoulders shrugged. "The name doesn't mean anything to me, Your Highness." He furrowed his brow at Durell. "Don't put too much weight on what he says," he told the emir.

Puzzlement darkened Sheik Zeid's sensitive face. "But this is authentic. It came from our archives."

"Ask him where that Israeli bitch is, Your Highness."

"What?"

"The Israeli agent, the spy."

Sheik Zeid swung his eyes back to Durell, and they looked black as an arctic night. "Where is the Israeli woman?"

Durell shook his head, scattering droplets of water. "It would only cloud matters if she were here."

"You're hiding her, so she can do more mischief."

"You have bigger problems now."

They stared at each other. Durell sensed that the sheik was judging him. He knew with a throat-stiffening dread that one word and McNamara would blast him. He did not think the word would come, but you never knew. You seldom knew anything for sure in his business.

Water dripped and gurgled.

The baths seemed totally deserted, and Durell reasoned that Sheik Zeid had bought the place for the night. It would have been the sensible thing to do.

Durell broke the silence. "Rest assured that the Israelis view you as the least of many evils, Your Highness. They believe you to be a reasonable and prudent man, and that's the most they dare ask." He took a short breath, and, since Sheik Zeid seemed disposed to listen, went on. "As for that document—I can't prove how General Abdurrahman got it, but Prince Tahir paid him a call earlier today. He may have taken it to him."

McNamara spoke to Zeid. "Maybe he was afraid it would be destroyed if things got out of hand in Dhubar, Your Highness. He was probably doing you a favor."

"After all," Zeid said with a nod, "it constitutes the legal basis for the regency in the event of my death. It should be protected."

"I have another idea," Durell said. "Maybe Prince Tahir and Princess Ayla stole the document and hid it for fear you might change your mind about who should be regent."

Sheik Zeid's cheeks hardened like desert bricks. His eyes went angry above tired blue smudges. "The prince and my wife have my fullest confidence, sir."

"There must be a reason why the commander of a Turkish armored division had that document," Durell persisted. "It could have gone to a bank vault for safe keeping."

"Surely there is a reasonable explanation."

"Don't count on it. I smell a conspiracy. McNamara lied to you when he said that I kidnaped Princess Ayla. Why did he do that?"

McNamara answered in a tone that was furious—a bit too furious, Durell thought. "It was a natural mistake, Your Highness, given the knowledge that Durell's so-called wife was a Jewish agent."

Durell spoke to the emir. "Here's something else to think about, then. McNamara attempted to have me killed in London."

"We knew the Israelis had reserved that room," McNamara replied. "Durell just happened to walk into a trap set for them."

"I don't buy that," Durell said.

"You don't have any choice," McNamara said, his sunburned face smug.

Durell looked at Sheik Zeid. "I have no liking for the ruthless world in which you men operate," the sheik said. "I prefer the contest of open arms. As undercover operatives, you men become like animals, preying on each other, trusting no one." He frowned. "There are many unanswered questions. My only interest at the moment is in finding my wife and assuring myself of her safety."

"Then you're a lovesick fool," Durell snapped.

"How dare you speak to me in that manner!"

"I'm being frank, because I want to help you. Has Princess Nadine told you where her daughter is?"

"She is a confused woman." Sheik Zeid sighed. "In time. . . ."

"There may not be much time." Durell's voice was grim. "If you go after Princess Ayla, you could get killed—for all you know, you're being led into a trap."

"What's to be done?" Sheik Zeid asked.

"More information would help," Durell said. "I know where we may get it."

The emir looked once more at the document of regency, then heaved a breath and said: "Very well. Colonel McNamara will accompany you."

"I don't need him."

"It pleases me to send him," Sheik Zeid said with a stubborn glare.

Durell thought of the oil the emir commanded, oceans of it, and every quart critical to the U.S. He made his tone bland. "All right," he said, "if you're willing to risk his neck."

Chapter 17

"You think Volkan is at your hotel?" McNamara asked.

"He could be, waiting to spring a trap," Durell said.

McNamara's shoulders were slumped beneath his brown

suit jacket, hiding their strength the way he hid everything about himself, as he drove from the *hammam*. Traffic was thin now, the air cool and damp as it came off the Sea of Marmara. Ships' lights made ribbons on the water down by the mouth of the Golden Horn, where vessels were lined up to await the early morning opening of Galata Bridge.

McNamara spoke dubiously. "I don't know—if he's really with Turkish Security, why would Volkan do that?"

"Because he's in Prince Tahir's pocket."

"But you don't have anything on Tahir."

"I don't yet."

A dissatisfied snort sounded from McNamara's blunt nose. His pale blue eyes showed an assertive self-confidence that hadn't been apparant in Dhubar. Durell sensed that he had overcome his earlier insecurity and found his footing with Sheik Zeid. He seemed to think he had everything under control—and maybe he did, Durell thought as they crossed the Horn and wound through the glowing tumble of old Istanbul on their way to Durell's hotel.

He was a highly competent man, all the more dangerous because you could never be sure what went through his mind.

McNamara broke the silence. "I regret our differences in the past, Cajun. I hope we can put that behind us."

"Do you?"

"Sheik Zeid was right to put us in harness together. We'll make a good team."

"You think so?" Durell said in a flat voice.

"I just wish I could say that about the pretty little chick you run around with." He cleared his throat. "You could show your friendship for Sheik Zeid by turning her over to us."

"You're out of bounds," Durell said. "I'm not that friendly."

"Don't get emotional. It's just business."

"You won't get the girl."

"What are you going to do with her?"

Durell ignored the question. They were almost to the hotel. "Better park here," he said quietly.

McNamara slipped his little Toyota up against a curb, switched off the ignition. The immediate neighborhood was still, except for heavy mood music from the Italian western showing in the garden cinema behind the hotel. An old man in baggy Turkish trousers that drooped between the legs shuffled by. Ships whooped and honked down below.

McNamara hadn't finished with Dara. "You know you've got to cut loose from her. I can't work with an Israeli; my people are her sworn enemies."

"You won't have to."

"If that's your answer, I'm not going any further," McNamara said flatly. "I'll have to return to Sheik Zeid and tell him you insist on sheltering that assassin."

"What are you talking about?"

"Didn't you know?" A slow grin spread across McNamara's cheeks. Then his face went angry. "She's been a member of a *Mossad* assassination team for four years."

Durell was stunned and dismayed. He wanted to reject McNamara's contention, but it added up.

Ever since London the thrust of her arguments had been that Princess Ayla was best eliminated. A cold sense of betrayal grew in him, but he was not convinced yet. "I was ordered to save the princess," he said. "It makes no sense for me to be teamed with an assassin."

"Maybe the Israelis had other ideas."

"Give me tonight. I'll talk to her."

"You'd better. Princess Ayla won't live ten minutes, if she gets to her first."

Durell felt a stab of anger, mostly at McFee for getting him into such a situation. He scanned the hotel from the car, blew an exasperated breath, and said: "Are we going to find out what Volkan has to tell us, or not?"

"Let's go," McNamara said.

The cramped little hotel was as dingy and scruffy as Durell remembered. They got out of the car, and the movie music heightened among baffling walls. As they crossed the street, Durell glimpsed the shadow of a man break away from the wall and twist soundlessly into the hotel doorway. He halted, flagging McNamara back, eyes plastered to the poster-framed entrance. Nothing more happened.

"He brought some help with him," Durell said.

"Looks that way." McNamara slid his gaze up and down the street. "Is there a back way?"

"Through that passage over there." Durell pointed to a narrow notch of deeper night.

"See you upstairs," McNamara said and faded into the darkness.

The twisting little street had no lighting. Its facades flashed as a trolley bus hissed past and threw sparks overhead. Shutters sealed away shops that heard, spoke and saw no evil, as Durell moved toward the hotel entrance.

The movie music rose in tempo and volume until it seemed to shake the stars.

Volkan normally was imperturbable, but tonight was different in many ways, and the music out there and the white shadows thrown by the cinema screen bothered him.

He wondered if he was doing the right thing—for he had reconsidered once again and decided to help Durell.

It had been a long time since he'd had to think for himself.

His mind returned to the summer *yayla,* where morning mists washed away down the valleys, and a nubbed sapling driven into the stony earth bore the crescented red flag of Turkey above his grandfather's tent.

In spite of his troubled spirit, Volkan's broad face smiled as he remembered his grandfather who told stories of the cunning Nasreddin Hodja, with a moral for everything. They had sat around the sparking campfire in the thin, chill air of a mountain night and consumed enormous quantities of rice and mutton wetted with yoghurt so that it squished between the fingers. They drank creamy *ayran* and had cheese pastries and grapes and melons.

Then, when the men were full with food and good humor, the adventure in their souls raised by wild stories, one, perhaps his uncle Kasin, would leap to his feet and perform a lunging, slashing sword dance while the others chanted.

Ah, thought Volkan, for the old days of youth and irrepressible courage and innocence.

To be a Turk. . . .

To fear nothing. . . .

How it must have thrilled, Volkan thought as he sat and waited in the darkened hotel room, to have heard with your own ears the Ghazi Pasha himself, as he commanded you to die for him, and to die willingly, eagerly.

There was something else his grandfather used to say— now, this was serious; how did it go? Volkan thought. He frowned below the black crescents of his mustache as he probed for the words: "You fight battles to win or be killed, God's hand holding yours wherever you end— back tilling your field or in Paradise!"

He would return to his village when this was over, when he'd seen it through, he decided. Perhaps he would be a school teacher—he had a university education, after all. He would spend his summers with his clan in the high pastures that remembered their nomad heritage, warriors come eons ago from Mongolia's Tian Shan Mountains to conquer the Arabs and the Byzantines.

A sickness of years was falling away from him, Volkan thought.

Let Prince Tahir try to dishonor him.

He would do the right thing—there was much, he realized now, that he might tell Durell. And then? Whatever Allah willed.

"Volkan?" Sadettin spoke quietly through the door.

"Yes?"

"He is coming."

Volkan sat still, and his eyes shifted back and forth across the darkened room. *"Tamam,* okay. Go to the men on the roof and wait."

Sadettin replied hurriedly. "Are you sure, Volkan?"

"What do you think? I'll call you when I want you."

"But—"

"Go!"

Volkan had not felt so good in a long time.

There was no sign of the lookout as Durell stepped with cautious care into the stone-floored lobby. The only light, behind the worn wooden grill at the reception desk, shone on a bald clerk who slumped dozing in his chair. A fitful fly crawled across his collar. Durell paused, surveyed the dim stairs ahead, glanced back at the street. The cinema out back made gunshot noises. Its music was a distant whirlwind of sound. Durell thought he heard applause.

He worked his way up the narrow stairs slowly, a step at a time, testing his footing against squeaks and groans from the old wood. The staircase smelled like a basket of dirty laundry.

He wondered who waited at the top.

He worried that McNamara might get lost in the blind alleys and snarled passageways behind the street.

He kept moving.

The dusky corridor was empty. A window at the far end brought in darkness. Durell scented a fume-laden dankness that drifted in from the streets and chimneys, the factories and shipping channels of Istanbul.

He thumbed back his coat and hefted the Marine .45 from his waistband, his flesh cooling at the belt where the heavy steel had sucked out sweat. The gun was down by his thigh, his breath light and easy, as he approached the door to his room.

He had expected a show here in the corridor, but nothing happened; maybe they were all in his room.

Certainly Volkan was not alone.

He looked back at the dark window once more, then stood fronting the door. There was no way to be clever about it, he thought.

His knee jerked up, and his heel slammed into the door near the old brass knob, and splinters flew and the door crashed inward with a rending, explosive bang. He crouched, darted, swung to the right, and dropped to a knee.

There was a moment of jaw-clamped silence as he waited, gun ready over the dim space in front, his vision adjusting on the gloomy hulk of Volkan.

"Don't shoot, Durell Bey."

"Show your palms." Durell spoke Turkish in a grating voice. He did not know what he had expected, but he had not thought it would be this easy. His nerves jangled at the thought of a trap closing behind him, and he slid side-wise to cover both the door and Volkan as the man gave a heavy breath and lifted his big hands. Seen through the window beyond Volkan's mountainous shoulders, the lights of Asia gleamed across the Bospo-rus. Then the Turk rose from his chair, and his bulk blotted out the window. He kept his hands raised shoulder high as he spoke with a loose peculiarity:

"You have nothing to fear from me."

"You didn't come back," Durell said through the gloom.

"I was afraid, but that was before."

"You have other men here, somewhere."

"Yes. Don't waste time, if you wish to evade them."

"Give me your gun. Easy."

Volkan's right hand came down slowly and slid under the lapel of his jacket.

Durell heard a thickness in his own voice, as he said: "I'm warning you."

"No need, Durell Bey."

Durell watched as the hand came back into view, the pistol held carelessly. An oddly disturbing smile crossed Volkan's lips. Then there was a swift motion behind him. A heavy thud shattered the smile, and Volkan's head pitched forward with a gush of breath; his knees thudded massively into the floor, and he pitched onto his face.

Durell's surprised stare found McNamara's snarling face. "That was unnecessary," he said.

"I didn't know you had him covered. He had his gun out."

"He was surrendering it."

McNamara's voice was apprehensive. "Where are the others?"

"They're here. Somewhere." Durell glanced through the door, where it hung by a single twisted hinge, then he stooped to the fallen Turk and spoke quickly. "Let's get him to the car."

"He's too big to handle on the fire escape," McNamara said.

"We'll drag him between us, like a drunk. Get a hold."

They draped Volkan's arms over their shoulders, and the huge form sagged between them as they struggled through the doorway. The glistening dome of the man's limply swaying head filled a corner of Durell's vision, and his toes grated along the wooden floor of the corridor, thumped after them in the dim stairway, dropping from step to step. The sound of Durell's breath clashed with that of McNamara's and made harsh echoes against the walls of the narrow staircase.

Durell kept expecting Volkan's confederates, but there was no sign of them.

"What did Volkan tell you?" McNamara gasped.

"Nothing." Durell sounded a bit puzzled. "But he seemed willing to cooperate."

"Do you think he knows where Princess Ayla is?"

"Could be—or something more."

"There's also the possibility," McNamara puffed, "that he would sell you some cock-and-bull story to mislead you."

"I'm aware of that," Durell said as they came to the bottom of the stairs. They hurried across the musty lobby, Volkan dragging between them. The clerk still was asleep. Outdoors, Volkan's toes trailed a grinding noise across the rough paving stones.

McNamara was soaked with sweat. He kept glancing down to where Volkan's head swayed from his loose neck.

The movie had ended, and a few of its patrons trickled into this street.

A shout came vaguely from the height of the hotel roof. Everybody looked up.

Durell saw no one, but he didn't have to. "They're up there," he said. He felt McNamara loosen his grip on Volkan.

"Let's drop him," McNamara said.

"No." Durell yanked toward the far side of the street

and almost threw McNamara off balance. "Get him in the car."

The pedestrians strolled on, the shout forgotten, oblivious to the apparently drunken trio crossing the street.

Durell clenched his teeth against the strain of Volkan's weight, cursed under his breath, raised his eyes again to the roof. The men would be hurtling down the staircase by now, he thought, and felt a spurt of urgency. He heaved to speed up McNamara, and this time the swearing intelligence chief tripped and went down on all fours. Volkan rolled away from Durell's shoulder and crumpled to the paving stones.

Durell bent and grabbed—and abruptly checked himself, startled by the sight of the tires on the Toyota.

All four had been slashed.

"Someone took precautions," McNamara said, on his feet now and hauling at the limp-jointed giant between them. His cheeks shone suddenly whiter in the pale radiance of the night. He started to say something else, but Durell cut him off.

"Around the back way. Quick."

They slogged back across the street in staggering tandem, the awkward weight of Volkan in the middle, and entered the dark passageway that McNamara had used before. They came out in the deserted space of the cinema, and Durell pulled toward a canted marble doorway with carved lintel and jambs that might have been a thousand years old. He had no idea where it led, but it didn't look like a dwelling entrance. Given the nature of the open area around them, which once might have been the courtyard of a palace or a caravanserai, it held out the hope of passages and chambers complicated enough to confuse pursuit.

A rushing footfall echoed from somewhere.

There were no more shouts.

Durell judged that the men had no wish to arouse the neighborhood and risk questions; they would be spreading out to search the immediate area quickly and thoroughly.

He wondered how many there were.

Then they were inside the marbled entrance, where they stumbled down worn, slippery stone stairs. The stairs twisted to the left, descended a bit more, halted in dank lightlessness. Durell felt chilled. The subtle fragrance of water touched his nostrils. He tried his penflash, but its tiny beam was too narrow and weak to be of much help, so he dug for a box of matches he always carried. The match sparked and flared, and its orange radiance was dimly reflected by water and marble columns.

"The place is flooded," McNamara said in a disgusted tone.

"No, it's an old cistern."

It was similar to the larger Yerebatan and Binbirdirek cisterns, both with hundreds of columns, the latter built during the Fourth Century in the reign of Constantine the Great, Durell remembered.

He thought he heard the men in the courtyard above as he surveyed as best he could the flat black water and twenty-odd columns that rose out of it to a vaulted brick ceiling. Where the walls were in reach were graffiti in numerous languages from countless epochs of history.

As he swung the diminishing match around, he saw that he stood on a clay floor that had been patterned with footprint on footprint.

McNamara spoke nervously. "They'll be in the courtyard by now."

"Keep your voice down," Durell whispered.

"We're at a dead end."

The match singed Durell's fingertips. He dropped it, struck another. He was aware of his thumping pulse, a dull ache in his wounded leg, as the slim flare trembled slightly in his fingers. He turned and regarded Volkan, who was sprawled on the wet earth. They had taken him as far as they could, he decided.

"Let's try to wake him up," he said. He cupped water in his hand and splashed it on the broad, mustached face.

There was not a stir.

He bent closer, pushed back an eyelid, felt a prod of anxiety that abruptly turned to rankling anger.

"He's dead," he said.

"After all of that?"

"You killed him, you son of a bitch."

McNamara's sweaty face went wooden, and his gaze probed Durell's eyes briefly before he spoke. Then he said in a flat voice: "You don't think I did it on purpose, do you?"

Durell felt the back of Volkan's head. Beneath the bruised flesh there, shattered bone felt like soggy straw. He considered McNamara's face by the light of the dying match. "You crushed his skull," he said.

"So—I've been deskbound. I'm rusty, lost my touch."

Durell said nothing, just stared at him.

"Why would I kill him?" McNamara protested. A chill drop of sweat fell from his round chin. "Maybe you thought I didn't want him to talk." His words quickened. "Maybe you think I'm in with Prince Tahir on some crazy scheme to—"

"To what, McNamara?" Durell's voice was low and even.

McNamara frowned. "You've got rocks in your head, Cajun," he growled. "He set a trap for you. Your first guess was right—what do you think those bozos are doing out there now? Waiting to shower us with rose petals?"

"They weren't in the room; he had them out of the way."

"Out of sight, you mean."

"It started as a trap, but I think he had changed his mind."

"Then you're a sucker."

Durell's left hand snapped his .45 from his waistband and pointed it at McNamara's gut. The match flame burned low and hot in his right.

The muscles lumped in McNamara's jaws. "What's that for?"

"We seem to be on different wavelengths."

"We can still be partners."

"Sure. I'm the partner that gets out of here alive."

McNamara's eyes widened a bit, then narrowed. "You're going to wipe me?"

"Maybe I should. I don't think you messed up Volkan's head like that by accident. But I need you." Durell gazed up at him, from where he crouched beside Volkan's corpse. The pistol felt heavy and awkward in his left hand.

"I thought you'd come to your senses," McNamara said. "You'll have to provide a diversion, so I can get away."

McNamara's face fell. "You can't ask me to do that!"

"Better you than me. Get up those stairs and run for it."

With biting quickness the match seared against Durell's fingertips, and there was a split second of pained astonishment.

It was all McNamara needed.

His toe smashed into Durell's chest, and Durell went back over his heels and sprawled into the rattling, ringing water. The black liquid filled his eyes and nose and brought a moment of near-panic when he was powerless to sense in the flat darkness of the chamber whether his face was above or below the surface. He harnessed his wits, rolled face down and gave an echoing kick that sent him diving as he jammed his .45 back into his waistband. He did not know if McNamara would try to shoot him, but he could take no chances, even in this utter darkness. Then he bumped into a stone column, embraced it to the surface, and took in a long, sweet breath. Water rolled down his taut cheeks, and his heart beat against his rib cage. There was nothing to show McNamara's presence.

Slowly he scanned the blackness above and toward the rear of the room.

McNamara's harsh whisper came from his right. "Hey, Cajun! Where are you?" A stifled breath of anger.

Durell kept his silence and twisted his face back and forth in hopes of catching the slightest radiance from some hidden source of light. The water was curiously sweet on his lips. He felt it dribble around his eyes and down his face.

Another whispered shout. "You're making waves in more ways than one, Sam. I'll let bygones be bygones if you will."

Durell lowered himself soundlessly into the water, aware that his wet .45 probably was useless, and stroked silently away from the direction of McNamara's voice until he found another column to grab.

"Sheik Zeid isn't going to be pleased," McNamara said.

Then Durell glimpsed a dim glow further back in the cistern and a few yards to his left. He studied it, ignoring McNamara's words. It had been simple enough to deduce that a cistern would have an inlet for its water supply. It could have been bricked over, of course, even buried beneath the foundation of some old building. But if that were the case, Durell had concluded, then the cistern should have dried up, its waters soaked into the soil over the centuries.

He felt reasonably certain that the faint radiance back there marked the water inlet.

He worked his way back, paddling quietly from column to column.

McNamara was still calling him, exasperation growing in his voice.

He reached the source of the glow and looked up and saw a steeply inclined brick tunnel just big enough to worm his way through. The scant illumination that came down from the street made glowworm-like marks on the eroded old bricks. A grating barred the far end.

Finding a handhold in the crumbling mortar, he pulled himself up, his shoulders popping with the effort. He swung free from the chest down for a long moment, and water splashed and gurgled out of his sodden clothing.

McNamara's voice became threatening. "What are you doing. You'd better get back here."

It was the last thing he heard McNamara say, as he took a breath, bunched his muscles, and heaved until he was in the brick pipe to his waist, with his feet still in the water. Another grip on the corroded bricks and he was fully inside, pulling himself up by bruised and skinned fingertips, pushing himself with toeholds gained in niches and hollows. When he scented the raw, rank odor of the streets above it was with a sense of gratefulness.

Bolts that had held the grating in place had long since rusted away. A couple of determined shoves and the grate clattered over, out of the way.

He crawled into the night. He was inside a low stone box that was open to the sky. A brick sluice came into the box from over two arches—all that remained of a Roman aqueduct. Houses built of trash and junk had been thrown up in the arches, homes of the poor in this forgotten, twisting alley.

His leg stiff and aching, Durell squished and sloshed away to find a taxi.

In spite of everything, he had a moment of misgiving about leaving McNamara to the dogs. But he put it aside. The importance of K Section's mission overrode all other considerations. And he had enough to think about as it was.

There was the possibility, however slight and incredible it might seem, that Turkish troops would invade Dhubar.

And that someone was attempting to lure Sheik Zeid to his death.

The thought of killing brought Dara to mind—had he been harboring the assassin of the very woman he was pledged to protect?

Had that been the Israeli plan all along?

Chapter 18

The safe house was on a lane that led from Gazi Muhtar-pasa Caddesi, beyond the Eyup Sultan Mosque with its bones of Mohammed's standard bearer and a footprint of the prophet himself.

Durell guessed enough people were looking for his footprints and glanced back as he followed the lane through a rocky defile.

Houses were plastered to the hillsides and filled the dells, jammed and crammed together like pieces of a puzzle, facing every which way in static disorder. Durell blew from his nose to clear the fetid odor of decaying garbage and untreated sewage.

This had been squatter country until it filled up some years before, land owned by the government and settled without permission by Anatolian peasants who migrated to the city or laborers returned from Germany with a bit of money and no wish to go back to their dusty villages. Once settled these sprawling slums became blocks of votes for the politicians, who promised to pave the streets and bring in utilities. Shops and cafes sprung up. The place took on an air of permanence. And other *gecekondus* —the word refers to a house built overnight without permission—kept the tradition alive, spreading from the edge of the city, raw and deprived and dangerous.

It was late now, nearly midnight. Dogs barked. Stars blazed in the cool sky, above a thin halo of city lights.

Durell stopped at a small house of whitewashed stone, tapped on its plank door.

"Who's there?" Dara's voice was indistinct, and Durell knew that she had kept a distance between herself and the door.

"It's me," he said.

There came a clatter at the latch, the door opened a bit, and Durell saw a bare lightbulb beyond her face.

"You look awful," she said as he stepped inside.

"It's been that kind of evening." He sighed. "Any problems here?"

"Only staying awake. I'm so tired."

"I may have been followed."

"You're soaking. Take off those clothes."

Durell glanced about the one-room dwelling. A neatly made pallet of quilts on a straw mattress filled one corner of the hard-packed dirt floor. A tin pipe rambled from a steel drum-stove across the open-beamed ceiling to vent through the wall. The low sofa and walls were covered with cheap factory rugs.

"Turn off the light for a moment," he said.

The light went out, and he pushed aside a window curtain. A slight noise she made as she came up behind him raised an unexpected welt of anxiety at the back of his mind. He did not turn his head.

He saw nothing to alarm him beyond the window.

The lane seemed empty.

The aimless barking of the dogs continued, fragmenting the eerie silence.

He pushed the curtain closed and felt Dara tug at his jacket, accommodated her, and the jacket slid down from his shoulders and off his arms.

He turned to study her face. It was the kind you saw on travel posters for beach resorts, he thought, fun-loving, sunny, and blithe, wholesome in a sexy sort of way. But now, by the waffling glow that came from the open-doored stove, he saw that it was wan and weary, the delicate fabric of her lightly freckled skin tight against flat cheekbones. Some vitality remained in her enormous hazel eyes as they lifted steadily to his gaze. It seemed incredible that she was a professional killer.

"Why are you looking at me like that?" She stood close and held the cold mess of his soggy jacket away from her.

Durell ignored her question. He shook his gaze loose and crossed the room and stood beside the hot drum of fire. He rubbed his hands together in the warmth of the jerry-built stove. "I suppose we can chance spending the rest of tonight here," he said. "Tomorrow we'll have to move again."

"I'm tired of moving. Let them come to us."

"Don't be so brave," Durell said with an edge of sarcasm, "or you won't last in this business."

"Volkan found us, and we turned him to our advantage, didn't we?"

"Volkan's dead."

Dara looked bewildered. "How . . . ?"

Durell told her what had happened as she draped his jacket over the back of a chair to dry, undid his tie, and unbuttoned his shirt. He finished and listened through the walls in the momentary silence that followed.

Then Dara said: "McNamara will be looking for you."

"That's nothing new; just another reason he's got."

She tugged at his shirt, saw the .45 under his belt, and reached to take it out.

"No!" Durell snapped.

She went back a step, her big eyes appraising his hard stare. "What's wrong with you?" she asked.

"Nothing."

"Is it something I've done?"

Durell kept his eyes on her as he nodded toward the rough-board cabinets in the cooking area. "See if you can find a cloth or some rags in there. I have to clean this thing," he said, and tugged the pistol from his belt and shook water from its barrel.

He was tired and chilled, although the barrel-stove had begun to warm him, and he was not in a very good humor. It was difficult to assimilate the winds of thought that blew across his mind as he sat heavily on the straw mattress, removed the magazine of the pistol, and inspected the chamber. He unfastened the recoil spring plug and broke down the weapon and began to wipe it clean with a cloth Dara dropped at his side.

She removed his shoes and set them in front of the stove.

Durell watched her without seeming to.

She sighed and said: "I want to take back what I said at the hotel last night. I suppose you've been thinking about that."

"Not much," Durell said.

"I have. When I said you didn't care about anyone else—that was childish of me. I know—I knew then—that you were doing your job; that it came before anything." She forced a thin laugh. "It's true of all of us, isn't it? If we have a small encounter, a moment of happiness or pleasure, then we should be grateful and leave it behind us with some grace. I'm afraid I'm guilty of wanting to hold onto what we had, so briefly, yesterday morning in London." She lifted her eyebrows. "Was it only yesterday?"

"Yesterday, long ago and far away," Durell said. He regarded her with solemn blue eyes.

"That's the problem," she said, and gazed at the earthen floor. "Looking, hoping—for something, someone to hold onto. I don't think you can understand. I admit it; I'm guilty."

"You'll have to give me some of your spare cartridges," Durell said. He had reassembled the gun. "I don't trust mine. That's the trouble with an automatic—a misfire can finish you."

Dara rose from her knees and went to her shoulder bag and withdrew a handful of heavy, clicking cartridges. Durell took them and reloaded the magazine of the .45. Dara had changed since London, he thought. She had softened perceptibly, and he wondered if the shock of Major Rabinovitch's death had influenced that. Perhaps it was just the continual, deadly pressure.

He did not know if it was more than superficial, this new tinge of feminine vulnerability that made him want to shelter her in his arms.

It could be only pretense—he lived in a world of deception and counterdeception, where even the truth, in carefully patterned cuttings, could be a fatal lie.

He laid his gun on the padded quilt next to his hip and shrugged out of his shirt. Dara hung it before the fireplace and came back with a towel and rubbed down his thick, black hair, then his scarred shoulders and chest.

She seemed happy to do this, and it felt good, and he did not interfere.

"Take off your trousers," she said.

He looked hesitant. A smile crossed her narrow, delicate lips. "Oh, don't be such a ninny," she said, and stooped to unbuckle his belt.

"You know, Sam," she said as she tugged at the buckle, "you are acting strange tonight. I can't see why."

Durell regarded her in silence as busily, with a distant objectivity, she gripped the cuffs of his trousers and pulled them off of his legs and carried them to the dry with the rest of his clothing in the warmth of the stove. When she returned, she studied the angry new blood on the bandage of his thigh-wound. "You should have that seen to," she said.

Durell took a deep breath. "Why didn't you tell me of your connection with *Mossad?*" he said in a stern tone.

There was no immediate answer, as Dara, kneeling now at his thigh, peeled the bandage slowly away. Blood was crusted around the stitches taken by the ship's physician in the Persian Gulf. "I hope this isn't infected. It could be dangerous," she said.

"Answer me."

She looked up at his eyes. "It's a lie," she said.

"What?"

"I have no connection with *Mossad.*" She held his gaze with quiet assurance.

"McNamara said you did."

"And you believed him?"

"In this case, yes. You've been all too eager to eliminate Princess Ayla."

He flinched as she touched the wound gently. A thin, cherry-colored fluid rose up shining in the gashed flesh. Two of his fingers lifted her chin.

"There is some truth in it," she admitted.

"How much?"

"I was assigned to a killer team until a year ago, first in Scandinavia, then Vienna, London, and New York." She shook her golden head. "I lost my taste for it."

"Did you really?"

"Cold-blooded killing, even of those who would exterminate my nation, just wasn't in me, Sam. I—I was horrified by some of the things. Of course, they were doing the same to us." Her eyes went sad and distant.

"You didn't look horrified when you killed that man in London. You've given the impression all along that you can't wait to do it again."

She replied in a low, earnest voice. "There is something that should be explained to you. You have such a monumental reputation, you see—did it ever occur to you that an agent assigned to work with you might feel inadequate by comparison? I bent over backwards to impress you, to show you how tough and determined and competent I was." She smiled forlornly. "I wanted your approval desperately. Perhaps I tried too hard—you said as much in London, when you told Ethan I was too eager, but I was so intent on earning your admiration that I couldn't see what was right under my nose. You were right. I was acting like a freshman."

"It makes a good story," Durell said.

"You don't believe me, then?"

"I don't know what to believe."

Dara's face went blank, as if he had thrown a switch, and she took a kettle from the top of the steel drum-stove and made tea.

He thought how she had been trained to dissimulate.

A good agent was capable of creating an almost impenetrable cover story from loose scraps of truth and fiction on a moment's notice.

The dogs had stopped barking.

Firewood snapped and fizzed in the stove. The air smelled lightly of woodsmoke and steaming clothes as he drank the strong, sweet tea from a hot cup and admired the feminine stride and twist of her body. She was pouring the rest of the scalding water over a wash cloth that lay in a chipped enameled basin. She came back to him in the dusky light and bathed his wound with the soothing cloth.

She broke the silence abruptly, her eyes on the task of cleaning his wound. "You must understand that my father and mother, and my brother, all my family, were killed by the Arabs. Revenge was all I thought about, really. I was crazy with it by the time I was recruited. Naturally, my superiors keyed on that—that aspect of my personality." She wiped tenderly at the angry wound, wrung the cloth into the basin. "I was finished and polished, taught how to walk and dress and kill, and then they sent me to take up duties under deep cover as a roving employee of a multinational hotel chain whose chief officers were sympathetic to our struggle. The life looked gay and glamorous, but. . . ." She shrugged. "You know what went on beneath the surface."

"And you requested transfer to more conventional intelligence operations?"

"I had met Ethan—Major Rabinovitch. He interceded for me, took responsibility for me. I don't think they would have allowed me to transfer otherwise." She looked up at him for the first time. "Do you believe me, Sam?"

"Maybe," he said.

She tossed the soiled bandage into the fire, tore a strip from a sheet, and made a fresh bandage for his thigh. With a last neat tug at a knot, she said: "You should stay off this leg for a while."

"Sure," Durell said dryly.

"That wound could incapacitate you."

"I've worked with worse."

"I see the scars." She ran a cool hand over the old injuries. "If your leg gets worse, I may have to finish this assignment for both of us," she said. "Could you trust me to do that?"

Durell regarded her briefly, then said: "Tomorrow, leave here early and post yourself outside Sheik Zeid's hotel. You'll tail him, while I make another try at winning Nadine's cooperation."

"Then you do trust me?"

"We'll try one step at a time."

She was close to him in the wavering light of the stove, her eyes wide and vulnerable, lips parted. Her presence was a palpitating, hypnotizing aura that enveloped him. They kissed, and he tasted the tea-sugared point of her tongue. Her trembling hand slid down the hard ridges of his belly as she murmured: "Love me, Sam, darling. Pretend, if you must. Just for a little while."

Durell studied the tender glow of her eyes, his fingers mingled in the fine blond hair behind her neck.

Suddenly he cocked an ear to the outdoors.

Her soft palm brought his cheek back around, and she smiled. "Forget the outside," she whispered. "Forget all but this room—this bed—us. . . ."

Durell embraced her.

It seemed a good moment for forgetting.

Chapter 19

The black Mercedes had been parked since midnight down the narrow lane from the safe house.

Dew beaded the dark polish of its body, and the man who sat behind its wheel had become cramped and querulous, wondering when the others would arrive. He understood the need for clearance—one did nothing without authorization from the top. And he recognized that additional men must be brought from a distance. Still, it seemed that they should have been here by now. It was four-thirty.

He fretted over his decision to allow the woman to leave unmolested.

But they had said Sam Durell was the prize.

Nothing else mattered half so much.

So, being only two men—he glanced sullenly at his sleeping partner—they had chosen not to chance losing Durell by taking the woman, who might have raised enough of an alarm to allow him to escape.

A repeat of his getaway from the hotel would be unpermissible. There would be severe penalties.

Something stirred in the heavy darkness of the slum, and the man glanced nervously about, his hand loosening the knot of his tie. A goat or chickens, he told himself. The *gecekondu* smelled like a latrine in a barnyard, he thought. He sat still in the darkness, and his strained red eyes watched the door of Durell's hideout.

Then two more cars parked behind the first, and a

dozen men stood in the chill night, whispering. Not a light shone in either direction along the stony lane. Nothing stirred in this last hour before dawn.

"Which one is it?" Sadettin asked. He spoke importantly. He was in charge now.

The driver who had spent the night on the lane pointed. "That one up there with the lopsided door."

"How do you know?"

The driver did not wish to admit that he had allowed Dara to pass, but there was no way around it. He shrugged and said: "A blond woman came out of there."

"You allowed her to leave?"

"She went the other way. It did not seem—" He was slapped and kicked on the shin. He did not object to that as particularly cruel. Discipline was discipline.

"Let's go and get him," someone said.

Another spoke up. "Be careful—remember what happened to Volkan."

"Volkan double-crossed us. He got what he deserved," Sadettin growled.

The black shadows moved quietly up either side of the lane. The men were nervous, excited. When Sadettin had stationed them to his satisfaction, he beckoned to one who carried a tin of gasoline. *"Çok iyiim,* very well, Adnan. Up on the roof. Pour it all over. Quickly."

"What if he doesn't come out? He could be overcome by the smoke," someone said.

"Then he dies," said Sadettin.

Dara had slipped out about four o'clock.

Durell had been dimly aware of the warm lobe of her breast beneath a nylon slip as she had dragged herself with reluctant slowness from his chest. A faint shuffling of fabric came from across the room where she slipped into her clothing, her lithe movements quick to avoid the cold. The click of the doorlatch had snapped the dreamy fog of Durell's dozing. He looked and she was gone. They had said nothing.

Dead embers lay in the cold stove.

Durell lay against a fading ghost of Dara's slender warmth, not quite awake.

Some time later he became aware of a sense of change. For a few long seconds he tossed irritably under the covers, his mind full of sleep. Then a waspish reek stung his nose, and alarms flared through him.

Smoke!

He lifted his eyes through a mist of searing fumes, comprehended the glare of fire that licked across the ceiling rafters, and his feet thudded against the floorboards. Sparks and flaming embers plummeted about him as he struggled into clothing that had dried and stiffened before the steel drum fireplace.

He suspected the fire was no accident. There was no time to consider it further, if he wished to get out alive. The bed was ablaze now, and its straw mattress sent up suffocating clouds of dense gray smoke that stopped his breath and singed his lungs. The place threatened to go up like kindling, floor, ceiling, and cabinets bursting into flame as the torrid air screamed and crackled.

Durell choked and coughed, sweated and stung in the hard, fierce glare as he held back another instant to toe into his shoes. And then he burst into the shock of cold night, pistol raised and ready.

He glimpsed a dark motion to his left, cut the other way, heard a cry.

Sadettin and another blocked his way.

Sadettin died in a heap, his brains scrambled by a slug from the .45.

A flicker of urgent footsteps, the flare of a yell, and heels slammed into Durell from above. He went down without seeing the man who had jumped him, his gun spinning through the air, his right shoulder numb. His knees struck the earth, and others piled on. He tried to say something about surrender, but it came out a pained gurgling as a forearm crossed his throat and crushed back his voice. He twisted, reached back, clutched a handful of greasy hair. Then something exploded behind his eyes, and he was sucked into darkness.

The strawberry sun rose above a fiery sea as a power cruiser in which Durell lay approached an island with forested hills. He shook cotton from his vision, rubbed a throbbing knot at the back of his head, ran a dry tongue over his lips. He was wobbly as he stared through the porthole. The sea was a flat calm. The vibration of the engine touched the soles of his feet through the teak decking.

He looked around.

He was confined in a small cabin. It was of triangular shape, under the bow, and the plash of the cutwater was clearly audible. He was alone, but he knew there was no way out, not yet. He did not bother to try the door.

The porthole brought in the red glare of the Sea of Marmara. Now a dawn breeze flawed the water's surface with catspaws as he studied the rounded land mass a few hundred yards away. He judged it to be one of the Prince's Islands, located just south of the Bosporus, a pleasure park for the tyrants of old as well as a place of exile and execution for innumerable Byzantine princes. Romanus Diogenes, an Eleventh Century emperor, was blinded and imprisoned there after being ransomed from the Seljuk Turks who had defeated him in Armenia at the battle of Manzikert.

Vanishing beyond a point of land was the harbor of a small fishing village, shops and teahouses crowded down to the water, white walls reflecting the dawn with thin, blown-glass hues. Then dark pines and high bluffs shut the morning light away.

The cruiser docked a few minutes later. The cabin door opened, and a man held a gun on Durell while another blindfolded him. It seemed rather late for such precautions. He did not resist or protest as he was led above deck and heard the hollow sound of his heels on the boards of a pier. Then gravel crunched underfoot. A mixture of pine resin and sea salt flavored the air. Reed warblers and robins mixed their morning song with the calls of ducks and gulls.

Rough hands guided him through a door into a hushed

interior where the air was still. There was a low exchange in Turkish. A cultivated and surprisingly high-pitched voice ordered the blindfold removed and addressed Durell in excellent English.

"You look rather the worse for wear, Mr. Durell. But then none of us has had much rest since you stole the document of regency last evening. Tell us where it is."

"It's in safe hands." Durell's tone was bland. His eyes adjusted to the soft lighting, and he found Prince Tahir's sneering face. Angry red glints of light in his black irises reflected the dawn that shone beyond a cypress-framed window. His lean body whispered in small, impatient fidgeting movements against the satin covering of an immense chair. He wore a long robe of brocaded silk and affected an enormous turban like the sultans of old.

Beside his chair stood a thick wooden staff. A large brass crescent, symbol of imperial Turkey, was recumbent at its peak, its needle-sharp horns pointed at the high ceiling.

Durell's eyes slid back to Prince Tahir. "How did you find out I took the document?"

"My man Volkan informed us that you had burglarized General Abdurrahman's house. General Abdurrahman at first told us that nothing had been taken. You were very clever. But a second inspection discovered the loss." A look of displeasure crossed his brooding face, and he lifted a narrow palm. "Does that satisfy you, Mr. Durell?"

"I suppose it has to." Durell paused. "What are you willing to pay for the document?"

"What would you ask?"

"Why don't you just go to the emir and get him to sign another one?"

"I am a wealthy man, Mr. Durell. I will pay you one million dollars."

"It wouldn't buy me much on the bottom of the Marmara."

The prince regarded him with a lifted brow and cynical smile. Only two of his men were in here with them, Durell noted, and they stood back a respectful distance. The large room showed riches in casual profusion, antique carpets, Iznik tiles, precious ivory, mother-of-pearl inlay, exquisite marquetry, Marmara marble.

"I shall guarantee your freedom, if you are worried for your safety, Mr. Durell. Your life is of no consequence to me, one way or the other. The money can be deposited in a Swiss bank today. My plans will bear fruit before you could obtain it."

"You have a tight schedule."

Prince Tahir nodded. "And you have interfered with it."

"So sorry."

The Ottoman prince's face darkened. "You do not appear to appreciate your situation," he said in his high, sinister voice. "I said your life is of no consequence—and you are obstructing events of the highest importance."

The bullet wound in Durell's thigh ached. He did not know how far he could trust his wounded leg. He thought of Dara and wondered if they had taken her after she left the safe house. "What about Dara Allon?" he asked.

"Ah. You've discarded the pretense that she is your wife. Good." He shrugged sleek shoulders. "We do not have her. She is unimportant."

"And your daughter—aren't you going to ask what I did with her?"

"We know you did not take her."

"I see. But you don't know where she is."

"Do you wish to sell me that information also? I have no need of it from you. I shall have it within the hour." Prince Tahir's long finger stabbed at Durell. "Only one thing. The document. It is worth one million dollars—and your life."

"I'll think it over."

Prince Tahir must have made a signal, but Durell did not see it. Something crashed savagely into the back of his skull, shattering his vision, and he found himself on all fours, dimly aware of his own ragged gasps as the prince's men kicked him. That first blow had rendered him almost helpless. His head reeled so that he could not have got to his feet even if they had let him. He was half blind, his ears deaf to all but a wild ringing and the sharp grunts of the men as they labored over him. He doubled up instinctively to save his bones and vital organs. They worked him over methodically, rhythmically, as if they knew how to inflict pain with a calibrated precision and impersonal care for the limits.

It seemed to go on, and on, and on. . . .

Chapter 20

Dara was puzzled.

Sheik Zeid had left his hotel alone, and she would have expected Pat McNamara at least to accompany him. Maybe McNamara had not been as lucky as Durell last night, she thought. For all she knew McNamara might be still in the cistern, dead and butchered. She gave a little shudder as she started her car. All the dying had begun to get to her. But it did not bother her half so much as the thought that you never knew when or how it would come to you. She remembered the look of terrified surprise on the faces of her victims. She shuddered again.

She was proud of her select profession. But after this mission, she would kill only in self-defense.

She was through with cold-blooded murder.

Except for one last hit.

She followed at a discreet distance as Sheik Zeid wove his black Mercedes through the first stages of Istanbul's commuter traffic, catching Kemeralti Caddesi and then hurtling northwest on Abdullezel Pasa along the bustling Golden Horn. The minarets of the ancient city's helmeted mosques were dusky blue pillars holding up an ivory sky as the faithful bowed toward Mecca and said their first prayers of the day. The calls of the muezzins were lost in the din of trucks and cars, boat and train whistles, the pounding clatter of the city's fevered awakening.

Sheik Zeid finally parked, and Dara sat in her car and waited to see what the short, muscular man would do. She scanned the neighborhood of small houses and shops. Looming above were the city walls, their gray stone battlements scoured and crumbled by the passage of some sixteen hundred years since they had been thrown up by Theodosius the Great. Later rulers had added two more walls on the outer side, beyond her vision, and it seemed no wonder that the defenses were not breached for a thousand years.

Sheik Zeid left his automobile and walked into a narrow lane that led toward the dark, weathered towers. Dara waited a moment longer, then followed. A donkey clopped by, pulling a water cart. A few people were on the street, sweeping sidewalks, gossiping, cranking down awnings. The tapping noise of hammers came from somewhere.

The emir slid into shadows beyond a stone portal. Dara hesitated, glanced over her shoulder, then went after him.

Inside the fortification a musty corridor turned, split, went up and down. Dara halted and debated. The tapping sound was louder now, overlain with voices. A stone clicked down a dusty staircase to the right. She watched the stairs, listened intently. The slap of climbing feet rewarded her patience.

She ascended cautiously and silently, face tilted to the higher shadows ahead. Then she was on a windowed landing where a beam of sunlight broke the gloom. The tapping and voices came from below now, and she looked out from the shadows. The sight below released tension that had been coiling in her with a springlike rush, and she gave a long sigh of relief. Turkish workmen were busily chipping away at the marble tombstones of a Byzantine graveyard, using them to manufacture the slabs that covered Turkish latrines with footprints carved into the marble.

A glance beyond revealed a breathtaking view of the spired city, the silver-flaked Golden Horn and peacock-blue Bosporus.

She was within shouting distance of the ruined palaces

of the Blachernae, residence of Byzantium's last emperors, near the little sally port called Kerkoporta, where the fierce Janissaries had penetrated Constantinople's defenses on that bloody May morning in 1453.

Somewhere nearby, Constantine Palaeologus, the last Byzantine emperor, fought to the death and went to an unknown grave.

Dara looked up the next flight of stone stairs and moved on with supple determination. She stalked with the single-minded purpose of a cat. There came the sound of a voice, and she checked herself.

"I'm sorry we had to meet like this, Your Highness." A regretful laugh. "I guess it isn't exactly your style."

The voice belonged to Nadine. It was strained, agitated, nearly unrecognizable to Dara. The emir said something, and Nadine's voice came back sharply. ". . . people watching me. Spying on me."

Dara moved two steps closer and heard Sheik Zeid say: "Were you followed here?"

"Could be. I don't think so, though. I think we beat them out of bed. At least that was the idea."

"You called me to Istanbul, then would not speak what was on your mind."

"I—I had to think some more. Sam Durell—"

"Did he interfere again?"

"Don't hold it against him."

"I do not trust him."

"He's tough, but he's on the level."

"He betrayed my man last night. Left him to a pack of wolves."

"He must have had good reason. He wants to help."

"He sows discord."

"He doesn't know the whole story, that's all," Nadine said.

There was a brief pause, and Dara heard the tinkle of a sherbet seller's bell, the crackling of magpies' voices. She smelled hot pastries and coffee from the street below.

Sheik Zeid's feet made a pacing sound on the stone floor.

Then he said: "You did not tell him the whereabouts of Princess Ayla?"

"I haven't told anyone."

"Not even Prince Tahir? Durell says your husband and daughter may be plotting against me."

"I'm scared of him," Nadine said in a pinched voice.

"Durell?"

"Prince Tahir."

"Nonsense."

"Ayla is afraid of him, too."

"What?"

"She made me promise not to tell him where she is; she made me promise not to tell you, either."

"Then perhaps she is afraid of me, too, silly woman."

Nadine sounded offended. "Look, Your Highness, I know my own daughter."

"Then tell me: has she gone mad to do this thing?"

"I don't know her reasons. She kept them to herself."

"Then perhaps she is plotting, as Durell said."

"Where is Sam now?"

"I do not know."

"I'd feel better if he could accompany you."

"Then you will tell me where she is?"

"Yes." Nadine's voice faltered. "Because I know you love her—and she needs someone."

Dara held her breath, her ears straining to hear, as Nadine's words came in a sudden rush. "She is at the home of friends in central Anatolia, near Göreme. Do you know it? Beyond Lake Tuz. . . ."

Dara listened and committed it to memory. When Nadine had finished giving directions and Sheik Zeid was reassuring her that he would make everything well again, Dara slipped quickly down the dusty stairs and ran to her car.

Her lovely face was grim as she gunned her car out of its parking space and rushed for Yesilköy Airport.

At last, for Israel, the princess was almost within her grasp.

"Are you ready to resume, Mr. Durell?"

Consciousness ebbed and flowed. Durell's extremities felt cold and numb as he rode with the tide, a scrap of flotsam in a universe that expanded and contracted. Lights winked, reeling mockingly as the sore pain of bruised and battered flesh awakened in his awareness. His head was full of the dark smell of bloody nostrils.

He lay still, taking his time.

"Answer me, Mr. Durell. Are you ready to bargain?"

The high voice of Prince Tahir raised a burning wrath in him, but he did not move. Each second that passed infused his tormented body with renewed strength, his mind with clarity of purpose.

He had to get out of here.

There came a thin clatter of china as someone replaced a cup in its saucer. Strong, fleshy fingers clutched Durell's face, craned it up from the prickly rug until his neck popped, and he flinched and a grunt escaped his bent throat.

He opened his eyes.

Prince Tahir's twisted mouth smiled scornfully at him. The man released Durell and stepped back, out of sight. Durell lifted his shoulders, head sagging down, rested a moment, then got slowly to his feet. Tahir still sat in the enormous satin chair, beside the pointed horns of his golden crescent standard. He sipped his coffee and studied Durell's face over the shell of his cup, and when he took the cup away his malicious smile showed a sparkling bead of coffee, like black venom.

Durell held back his fury.

Prince Tahir spoke in a reasonable tone. "I offered you one million dollars for the document of regency, before your, ah, unfortunate—"

"Make it five," Durell snapped.

"Five?" The prince's eyes narrowed to thoughtful slots. "Five was rather more than I had expected to pay. However. . . ." He nodded his agreement.

"Ten?"

"Do not toy with me, Mr. Durell, I warn you." His lean body stiffened angrily. Violence was in the air, its electric odor thick in Durell's awareness. He knew he was pressing his luck, but that was what he had to do.

He said: "What difference does it make? You'll agree

to any price, because you have no intention of paying it. Once your hands are on that document, I'm a dead man."

"There is such a thing as honor among gentlemen."

Durell spoke bluntly. "A gentleman wouldn't scheme to kill his šon-in-law. You need that document because you are afraid Sheik Zeid may have second thoughts about signing another like it. You took it out of the country to make sure he did not destroy it in your absence, while you came to find your daughter. It's the key to your whole plan."

"And what plan is that?"

"To kill Sheik Zeid and rule his country from behind your daughter's throne," Durell charged. "You will use Turkish troops to shore up her regency, if necessary. That's where General Abdurrahman comes in—with or without the sanction of his superiors and the Turkish government."

Prince Tahir's swarthy face paled, then flushed, and rage bulged his black eyes. "Yes, and that will not be all." His voice became cunning. "Once Dhubar is in my grasp, I shall bargain its billions of dollars, its immense oil reserves for a military coup that will restore the Ottoman ruling dynasty to its rightful throne. Of course, a person of your utter insignificance can hardly be expected to comprehend the injustice done my family." A vengeful glitter lighted his eyes. "But no measure is too stern, no path too bloody to keep me from rectifying it."

He gazed beyond Durell, abruptly solemn, as if contemplating the vision of the founder of the Ottoman imperial line. Sultan Osman, legend said, had seen the horns of a crescent moon grow until they encompassed the limits of his future empire.

"From the wealth of Dhubar will spring the beginnings of a new Ottoman Empire," he breathed.

"And new slavery for the Arabs and Jews."

Prince Tahir's charcoal brows dipped between his scowling eyes. "The terrible Turk, as you westerners called me, will reclaim what is his."

"What about the superpowers?"

The prince's chuckle was dry as an Anatolian gully.

"They are like our musclebound Kirklareli wrestlers, locked together in holds of suspicion and fear. They heave and groan, but nothing much happens. By the time they disentangle themselves, it will be too late. We shall overcome all difficulties."

"You're crazy."

Tahir was fidgeting again. "My patience has worn thin. I had not expected these delays. Where is the document?"

"I don't have it."

Prince Tahir sat up, his mouth warped with rage. "Tell me, or I'll see you skinned alive."

Durell sensed the approach of the guards as they moved up behind him. He knew he had played out his respite. "There won't be time for that," he said, his face calm. "The others will arrive any second."

"Others?" The prince's eyes widened. "What others?"

"Turkish Security, of course." Durell bluffed with a grin. "You don't think your men took me without me wanting them to, do you? There's a homing transmitter in the heel of my shoe."

The prince looked stunned.

Durell took the instant before he recovered to lunge for the staff that held the brass crescent emblem. He heard a commotion and knew the two guards were bounding after him from their positions at the rear. He took no time to look at them but yanked the staff from its heavy base plate and stabbed its butt blindly and viciously backward. It smashed into someone, jarring his wristbones, and he heard a howl, spun, saw the heavier of the two bent double.

The smaller one came on, clawing for his gun.

Prince Tahir leaped from his chair, his dark face swollen with wrath.

In one sweep of lightning motion, Durell slammed the blunt end of the staff across Tahir's chin, then made a thrust of the wicked crescent tips that ripped out the smaller guard's throat.

The man sank to his knees as panic bloated his eyes, and his fingers scrabbled at a jagged rip in his neck. Blood and breath spewed and babbled.

Tahir was out cold.

The larger guard was still bent double, gasping through a wincing face, when Durell mercilessly broke the heavy staff across the back of his skull.

"And then there were none," he muttered with some satisfaction. "Uh-oh, spoke too soon."

Another man appeared in the doorway, his face alarmed by the ruckus. Durell threw the double-pointed brass crescent like an ax, and its horns thudded into the man's chest. He screamed, tumbled away.

Durell scooped up a fallen Beretta automatic, ran and burst through a cypress-framed window. He hit the yielding turf in a glassy shower, came up on the balls of his feet, and sprinted through the pines. Shouts and bellows echoed from inside the mansion.

His thigh was stiff, and a red stain seeped into the cloth of his slacks above torn sutures. The wound burned and complained. He gritted his teeth and kept going, his eyes on a shiny speedboat moored down the shallow slope.

Now came the spiteful snapping of gunfire, and a twig fluttered down in front of him.

Then he was out of the pines and in the sky's white glare. The sea was starkly blue. He crossed a pebbled beach to a floating dock, hurled himself into the rakish launch and cast off as slugs spanked the water.

A thirty-foot power cruiser was idling up to its moorings as half a dozen men burst shouting from the house. Durell watched over his shoulder as it swung around and gave chase, but it was too slow. Ten minutes later it was reduced to a white speck in his wake and turned back to the island.

A bone-wrenching half-hour went by as the light boat crashed from wavetop to wavetop, then he was in the Bosporus between the Haydarpasa railway station on the Asian side and the enigmatic walls of Istanbul on the European. He cut across the bow of a sparkling white ferry, overtook a Lyle tramp steamer with its maroon hull and yellow funnel, then angled toward Nadine's *yali*.

A few moments later he docked the boat and entered

the house through a door that stood open to a ground-level sundeck.

A house fly buzzed and batted against a window.

The efficient hum of a refrigerator came from the nearby kitchen.

The house seemed empty as he moved through warm, silent rooms. But then he heard something else. It might have been the scrape of shoe leather, a gasp, he did not know. His hand went under his jacket to the Beretta in his waistband as he stopped, listened, went on.

The sundeck door puzzled him. It did not seem likely that Nadine would have left it open.

He whiffed expensive cologne, then the burnt odor of dead embers as he turned into the sitting room. Draperies blocked a sun that struck hotly now against streets and heads and steel decks of ships. A mound of cold ashes filled the domed fireplace, as if Nadine had sat up all night—the fireplace had been clean the day before.

There came a broken, panting sound.

Mirrors around the room reflected his soiled clothing and taut face as it swung back and forth. Then he stepped around a sofa, and there was Nadine.

She was hardly recognizable.

Her perfectly shaped face was distorted by angry blue lumps and swellings, the dazzling platinum hair matted in bloody tangles and cords. A sleeve of her dress had been ripped off, buttons popped loose. A massive bruise blemished the pendulous whiteness of her exposed left breast. A flutter of eyelashes showed the incredible blue of her irises as he gently tugged the hem of her dress down. He did not know what they might have done to her, but he judged by her eyes that she had told them all they wished to know.

She whimpered as he laid her on the sofa. "Oh, Sam—I screwed everything up."

"Just take it easy."

"Can you forgive me?" she asked through swollen lips.

"For trying to protect your daughter? Nothing to forgive." He worked each elbow and knee, then moved firm, probing hands down the slender width of her rib cage. She sucked in a sharp breath. "You'll be all right," he said. "A rib may be broken. I'll call an ambulance."

He started for the phone, and her small hand gripped his wrist. "It was Prince Tahir's men," she said.

"I guessed," he said. He remembered the cabin cruiser he had encountered as he fled the island and Prince Tahir's boast that he would know Princess Ayla's whereabouts within the hour. "I passed them on the way," he said.

"I had to tell them where she was. They just kept knocking me around." Tears welled into her eyes. "It seemed there was no end to it."

"Don't get excited."

"I had just told Sheik Zeid."

"So he and Prince Tahir will be headed for the same place. That will fit Tahir's plans perfectly." Durell chewed on his lip.

"Do you think he would harm Sheik Zeid?"

"We may have a brief grace period," Durell said. "Prince Tahir has to have possession of a certain document before he makes his move. The trouble is, Sheik Zeid has that document, and he doesn't believe that Tahir and Princess Ayla are threats."

"Sam! You don't suppose—that Ayla is in this with Prince Tahir?"

"I don't know."

She held his darkening eyes with a pained gaze as an apprehensive shiver seized her. "No! I won't believe it," she moaned.

"Then why is Ayla hiding?"

"It's beyond me. She made me promise not to tell anyone where she was, not even Sheik Zeid—but I told him anyhow, because I *know* they love each other."

"I just remembered something—Dara was to tail Sheik Zeid this morning."

"Your wife?"

"She isn't my wife. She's an Israeli intelligence agent."

"I don't understand. Everything is crazy."

Durell blew a short breath through his nose. "I owe you the truth," he said. "She may be a killer."

"You mean she might—she might. . . ." The words stuck in her throat.

Durell nodded.

"Ayla?"

"Yes. And if she overheard your directions to Sheik Zeid, she's already on her way there."

Nadine's face went white. "I've been such an ass. If only I'd told you yesterday—"

"Don't waste your breath," Durell interrupted. "Tell me now."

Chapter 21

A roadblock had been thrown across the dirt road that wound along the wavering edge of the valley of *peribacasi*, "fairy chimneys," the weird natural pinnacles of ancient Cappadocia.

Durell had cut off from the asphalt highway between Urgüp and Göreme in central Turkey, following Nadine's careful instructions, and had expected to come in about three kilometers to the white stone house where Princess Ayla hid.

He had gone little more than a kilometer when he glimpsed the barricade at a twist of the road about five hundred yards down the scrubby, rocky slope. Two soldiers armed with automatic rifles stood down there. He killed the engine of his green VW, glided into a graveled nook beside the trail, and decided regretfully that he must cut across the low ridge on foot.

The sun was blistering, but a breeze up here helped somewhat. At the crest, he squinted across the glare for the roadblock, but it was hidden behind ridges and out-croppings. To his rear the snowcapped volcano, Erciyes Dagi, sparkled against a radiant sky. The ashes it had spewed in the Tertiary Age had become soft tufa stone from which eons of weather had carved the white, pink, and yellow spires that spread across the bleak landscape below.

Greek Christians hiding from raiding Arabs, Mongols, and Turks had found refuge in these weirdly needled valleys, Durell recalled. For a thousand years they had chipped and scraped and bored in the earth, hollowing out cavern churches, monasteries, even whole villages stocked with the necessities of life to house them in times of invasion.

The dusty, savage land seemed incapable of supporting human habitation, but he could look down on a small village heaped in a narrow valley. Poplars grew dark and green along a dry watercourse. Apricots lay drying in the sun on flat rooftops. Veiled women strung washing.

It was a peaceful scene, and he would have liked to rest here, but that would only stiffen his leg and remind him of its pain.

Besides, there was no time.

After calling an ambulance for Nadine, he had contacted Rob Thawley at the consulate, and Thawley had reported that General Abdurrahman had rejoined his division on Cyprus during the night. His troops had embarked on transports, ostensibly for normal rotation back to Turkey.

But an NRO satellite showed that the transports were holding station in the Mediterranean rather than steaming for home.

Durell had hung up convinced that the armored division only waited for Prince Tahir's signal to swing southward for Suez and Dhubar.

Burdened with an overpowering sense of urgency, he had chartered a plane for Kayseri, where he had rented the VW.

He might have been too late already—and now the roadblock stole more precious time.

His thigh wound burned and throbbed as he made his

way down the slope and along the limit of the valley of fairy chimneys, his gait a stiff, swinging limp. Sweat rolled down his cheeks and spattered in the thirsty soil. The road came again into view on his right. He kept his distance from it, even though its smoothed surface would have eased his way. With a game leg he could not afford to be surprised where the route twisted and dipped among outcroppings and ravines.

He glanced back, listened, perceived nothing to show that the soldiers at the roadblock suspected his presence.

A lark warbled.

The air was redolent of wild herbs, and the sky looked hard as lapis lazuli, infinitely high and melancholy.

He dropped prone in the scrub as a farmer rode a donkey around a bend, straddling the animal between two deep straw baskets, his scuffed shoes flattened at the heels to avoid the effort of tying and untying them. Durell was tempted to bargain for the donkey, but the farmer might say something to the soldiers about it. He let the man pass, and when he had clip-clopped out of sight, Durell hauled himself up and told himself that he must go on. The torn thigh must be made to function as long as possible.

There was dark, damp scarlet in the gray dust where he had lain.

He hobbled on under the brazen sun, his pace slow through the clutching scrub brush. The sere land dipped and heaved, each change in grade a challenge.

A high fang of stone rose above the close horizon of the next hill. Its surface was scraped and chiseled, a score of dark cave openings staring out of its steep sides. Then he topped the rise and saw more spires and cliffs that had been honeycombed with tunnel entrances.

To his left, on a sloping shelf of alluvium, was the country estate of Dr. Kemal Köse, if Durell had his directions correct. A vineyard stretched down its rearward slope; big leaves danced in the hot breeze, tossing the light of a lowering sun. Lemon trees and poplars shaded the grounds.

Nadine had said the house was vacant for the summer, except for Princess Ayla.

It would be crowded enough now, Durell thought.

A pair of helicopters was parked on the lawn. They bore the star and crescent insignia of Turkey. They were painted dark green, and Durell took them for military aircraft, remembering that the home base of General Abdurrahman's division was an army post in this region of Cappadocia. A handful of soldiers lounging in the shade must have come from the skeleton garrison remaining at the post, he reasoned.

A needling impatience gripped him as he glanced at the sun. Sunset was still half an hour away, but he'd better not wait if Prince Tahir had Sheik Zeid down there. He spared a thought for Princess Ayla, but she was secondary at the moment.

As for Dara—he couldn't afford to worry about her now.

Until Sheik Zeid was out of danger, no one else counted, including himself.

He studied the layout and decided his only choice was to work his way down into the valley below the house and come up to it through the sheltering rocks and then the vineyard. It was a long way around. He sat on the warm soil and ripped his trousers open above the oozing wound. His thigh was caked with blood. The flesh was tender and inflamed, and shooting pains raked out when he touched it.

He got to his feet, aware with sudden concern that he was nearing exhaustion, and stumbled on down the slope. He was a man of bullish stamina, his body conditioned by years of hardship, and he had a driving determination that left little thought for personal discomfort or the frailties of flesh and bone. There was something to relish, he had learned, in the mastery of will over body that seemed to call forth reserves of strength from an almost mystical source.

He slipped and plodded.

He kept going somehow, pressed on by the loom of impending disaster, images of violence floating before his mind—Sheik Zeid bloodied and dead; the Mideast in flames; and the flames spreading and spreading. . . .

He stopped suddenly, tall form wavering a bit, ear cocked.

Someone was weeping.

He turned his face up the steep slope as his eyes followed hand-hewn steps in the soft rock face. He wound his way up, and the sound grew louder. He came to a tunnel entrance, hesitated briefly, slid inside, the fingertips of his left hand trailing along the wall.

There came a tight gasp, then, in English: "Oh, no! Please—please don't!"

Durell's eyes found Princess Ayla, crouched in a nook in the tunnel, her beautiful face wet with tears, and he realized with abrupt consternation that she was speaking to him.

"Don't kill me," she pleaded.

"I won't harm you," he replied, his tone soothing.

She wore boots and riding britches, and her long, raven hair was done in a chignon that had loosened. He read disbelief and horror in her black almond eyes. "Your wife. . . ." she sobbed.

"Dara isn't my wife," he said wearily.

"Then why . . . ?"

"There isn't time to explain. What did she do?"

The words came in a rush. "She shot at me! She's after me—if I hadn't known these caves and hills since childhood, she would have—oh!" She buried her face in her hands, then wiped her palms back across her slick cheeks. "I was horseback riding." Her voice strained against grief. "She killed my horse; she killed Omer!"

Durell's eyes swept the vista beyond the cave. He spoke calmly. "Do you know where she is?"

Princess Ayla waved vaguely. "Out there, somewhere." She shivered violently. "Please, don't let her—"

"I won't."

"Why would she do this to me?"

"She thinks she has reason enough." He drew a thoughtful breath. "Your father's down there at the house, isn't he?"

"Yes. I saw him arrive."

"He may have Dara now. Why haven't you gone down?"

"I can't—I mustn't!"

"You know Sheik Zeid is there, perhaps in danger?"

She bowed her head. A stick of soft, shiny hair fell past her smudged cheek. "I would only make matters worse," she said softly.

"You'll have to tell me about that, later. All of it."

A tear from her downturned face made a mud pearl. "I. . . ." She shook her head.

"You'll have to." He moved on his knees to the edge of the cavern. The sun rested on western hills now, its low rays washing the countless stony spires with muted hues of pink and amber. Threads of purple dusk lay through the valleys and gorges.

"What are you going to do?" she asked.

"Give me your bracelet," he said, and extended a hand. She did not ask why, surprising him. He felt the twisted band of gold and rubies in his palm, turned, gave her a nod. Behind her, where the cave widened into a chapel carved from the living rock, a carved-out window brought twilight beams shining against primitive wall and ceiling paintings of saints and emperors long dead.

"My father gave me that," she said and indicated the bracelet.

"Good."

"Is that your price for protecting me?"

Durell felt sorry for her, then closed his mind to it. "I don't want your jewelry," he said. "I'm only borrowing it."

"I don't know why I trust you," she said.

"Any port in a storm."

He got to his feet. Pain hammered in his thigh, and he felt sweat on his forehead. "I'm going down now," he said. "Keep out of sight."

The first stars winked in a sky of ivory and roses as he limped down the weathered stairs and came out once more in view of the house, beyond the sloping vineyard. It seemed peaceful in the lull of dusk, but the cooling stillness held the ghosts of countless warriors—Hittites, Phrygians, Cimmerians, Scythians, Persians, Greeks, and

Romans, just to count those who had fought here before the beginning of the Christian era.

Durell supposed more ghosts would be added tonight. He hoped his would not be one of them.

He made his way up through the leafy vineyard, left leg dragging, jaws clamped tightly. A day had passed since he had eaten, but he felt no hunger, just a slight nausea at the top of his stomach. He knew as he worked his way through the settling dusk that the odds were implacably against him. But the consequences of failure ruled just as stubbornly against turning back. Disabled as he was, his best hope lay in avoiding physical stress. He was aware that there could be no repeat of the quick agility that had gained him freedom from Prince Tahir that morning.

He had the Beretta—and his hand slid to the comforting reassurance of its grip—but it was outclassed by the automatic rifles he had seen in the soldiers' hands.

Brains, gall, and luck were the only weapons that would count for him now.

There came a sudden crash.

He checked his limping stride, peered from among the grape vines. There were muffled shouts. Nothing else happened for a moment, then the dark figures of men appeared among the trees around the building, and Durell threw himself flat against clods and weeds. The impact jolted a grunt out of him, and he cursed, wondered how much longer he could last on that leg.

He waited.

Crisp shouts cut the twilight; the tread of boots came down near the vineyard. Scraps of Turkish came to him: someone had broken out of the house.

The search moved away, and he rose shakily, took a deep breath, looked right and left.

Momentarily he was exposed, a hobbling figure crossing a space of lawn behind the house. But his luck held. Then he was beside the wall, bent awkwardly below the windows as he moved past. Birds settling for the night in lemon trees made a high-pitched racket. The green fragrance of a vegetable garden came from somewhere.

He was in the grip of a pulse-pounding urgency.

Someone had escaped, and Prince Tahjr would be in a towering rage. If he still held Sheik Zeid, the little emir's life span might be measured in minutes.

Then a hand touched Durell's shoulder, and the hair went stiff at the nape of his neck. He spun, nearly going down on the weak leg as he reached for his Beretta.

"Easy!" came a stiff whisper.

And out of the shivering leaves of a dusty shrub rose the drawn face of Patrick McNamara.

"He was going to kill me—Sheik Zeid, too." Blood dried around a gash on McNamara's cheek, where he had gone through a window.

"Zeid's still in there?"

"I'm afraid so." McNamara looked scared. "You have transportation?"

"We can't leave him."

"You think I want to? But there isn't a prayer of springing him."

Durell did not care for McNamara's attitude. But he guessed he could trust him after all, if Prince Tahir's men were after him. "There's a chance," he said. "I've got the princess."

McNamara's face changed in the dim light, and some of the fear went out of it. A bit of color returned. "Where is she?" he asked.

"What about last night, in the cistern?"

"Self-defense, Cajun. They would have killed me if I had run out of there like you told me to."

"How did you get out, then?"

"I found your way out. I knew you weren't harmed—I hadn't kicked you hard enough. Is all forgiven?"

"I can use you," Durell said for a reply. "Do you have a weapon?"

McNamara showed his chopped .45. "My baby. I got it back from the dope who was guarding me."

Durell twisted, pointed out the dark bulge of a hill that rose from the right rear quadrant of the estate. "Princess Ayla is in the top tunnel. There's a staircase cut in a low rock face, beginning about halfway up."

"She's alone?"

Durell nodded. "She'll be glad to see you."

"What about that Israeli babe? I thought you were inseparable."

"She's somewhere around here. Look out for her. Tell Princess Ayla we will pick her up in a helicopter shortly."

"You have a plan?"

"Just have her waiting on top."

"Yo. I'll snatch a flashlight from one of the choppers on my way."

"Take care."

The big man pushed out of the snagging shrubbery, bent double, and darted into the gathering darkness. Durell quickly surveyed the area, saw that the soldiers had returned from their search for McNamara and were resting by the road that ran in front of the house. Apparently McNamara didn't count for that much and could be left to the wilderness for the moment.

He hobbled painfully along the side of the house, hoping to make the front door without being seen. Then, as he passed a window, a muffled snarl of angry voices caught his ear. He looked inside, saw Prince Tahir. One of his men stretched a shining red cord between his fists and strode across the room to where two others held Sheik Zeid.

They were preparing to strangle him.

Chapter 22

Durell lurched for the door, a scant two yards away, drove through, and found the lethal cord already looped around the sheik's neck.

Everything stopped.

The room was full of stares.

The staccato chitter of birds came from the lemon trees. Then something else—the clatter of soldiers' boots. Durell's slamming entry had aroused them, but he'd had no choice in the matter. He kept his hand away from his gun as they tumbled in behind him. He held the eyes of Prince Tahir's livid face momentarily, its twisted lips skinned back warningly from long teeth. He felt rifle muzzles against his back as he regarded Sheik Zeid. The emir's sensitive brown eyes showed no fear, only an offended sense of dignity.

Prince Tahir recovered his composure and said: "If you came to save His Highness, I'm afraid you are a bit late."

"I'd say I was right on time."

"But you seem to have forgotten your weapon."

"I don't need a gun."

"Oh?" The prince's mouth twisted into a condescending smile. "You have no authority, no arresting power. You are too clever to suppose that I would surrender if you did. What—?"

"All I want is the release of His Highness." Durell's tone was blunt. "The Turkish authorities can take care of you." He noted the sullen blue lump his blow that morning had raised on the prince's chin.

"It will be too late for them to stop me by the time they find out."

It was the kind of answer Durell had hoped for, since he hadn't been sure whether the government was in on Tahir's conspiracy. "Your plans won't work," he said. "Not without the document of regency."

"I have that."

Durell swung baffled eyes at Sheik Zeid. The emir nodded sad affirmation, and said: "But I don't know how. . . ."

Prince Tahir's high voice sneered. "This is no gamble, you see. I win—you are dead. Both of you will be eliminated. The silken cord used by my ancestors is reserved for persons of high birth, however. You, Mr. Durell, will be shot."

"What about Princess Ayla? You won't get anywhere without her, will you?"

"She must be in the vicinity."

"I have her."

"Do you? We will find her after we have disposed of you."

"Think again. I left her in the custody of Dara Allon—remember the Israeli intelligence agent?"

Red spots of fury flickered in Prince Tahir's eyes. "You are lying!" he shouted.

Durell kept his face bland. "Miss Allon will kill her, if I don't return in"—he made a show of reading his wristwatch—"ten minutes." It was a bluff, but its credibility was written all over Tahir's lean face. "Do you doubt that Miss Allon would do it?" he goaded.

Prince Tahir looked around at his men, seeming briefly at a loss. But their blank faces showed no reassurance, and Durell suspected they didn't even understand English. Then his murderous gaze came back to Durell, faltered, steadied with decision. "No. I won't believe it. You are desperate, trying to deceive me. . . ."

He stopped in midsentence.

Durell was holding out Princess Ayla's bracelet.

"Ah. Ah, well." Prince Tahir looked stunned.

"Time's running," Durell said.

"Very well. You may take Sheik Zeid, but you will never get away from here alive." His voice took on a burring edge. "Once you pick up Princess Ayla, you must cross several kilometers of open country. You will be exposed and vulnerable. I can wait a bit longer." He gave a Turkish command, and the silken cord was taken from the emir's neck.

"You're checked out on helicopters, aren't you?" Durell asked Sheik Zeid when they were outside.

"I have flown almost everything."

"Good." Durell led the way to one of the aircraft. "Prince Tahir won't be expecting this. We'll have to make it quick, or he might have a change of heart. Get in and start it up."

Sheik Zeid looked dubious. "I won't leave without Princess Ayla," he said.

"We'll pick her up on top of that hill over there." Durell pointed through the gloom. Night had filled the land now and left only the pale golden snows of Erciyes Dagi suspended above the darkness. The first stars seemed an arm's reach away in the dry, clear air. Durell's burning thigh made his leg a stiff, alien weight to be dragged into the helicopter with him. His jaw muscles trembled, holding back the pain. A raw urgency rubbed his vitals as Sheik Zeid went methodically through a preflight checklist.

"Forget that," Durell spat. "Get this thing in the air."

"Yes. You are right," the tense man replied.

Just as the first muted whine of the turbine sang from the machine, there came across the empty darkness a flat, slapping echo.

Both faces snapped toward the hill where Princess Ayla was to have waited.

"Someone is shooting up there," Durell said.

"My God!" Sheik Zeid blurted.

As if released by a spring, men tumbled out of the house. There was another shot, and some darted in the direction of the firing. Others, visible in the low light flung from windows, dropped to a knee and swung their weapons toward the revving helicopter. Just as it leaped into the air, Durell glimpsed the orange wink of muzzle blasts and tried to make himself smaller. The thump of slugs came to him through the ship's shuddering frame. A burst stippled the windscreen and scattered flakes of plexiglass. Then the hill came up fast and black, and the blood pounded at his temples like the clapper of an alarm gong.

No one waited on top.

He could not guess what had happened in the cave, but there was no time to wonder.

He'd have to go in and find out.

"Don't land," he shouted over the scream of the turbine. "Hover low, so I can jump. Then beat it." He found a flashlight between the seats, looked back, saw lights of

Tahir's men as they scrambled through the vineyard toward the hill.

"I said I would not leave without Princess Ayla." Sheik Zeid glared stubbornly through the radiance of cockpit lighting, hands and feet delicately working the helicopter's controls.

"You must save yourself for your country, Your Highness. It comes first."

Durell tumbled out, hit the ground, sucked in a breath as sharp pains stabbled from his thigh into his groin. The angry light of electric torches danced up the slope toward him. Sheik Zeid's indecision was evident in the momentary hesitation of the aircraft. The men below paused to fire, and slugs thumped and drummed and whined. Durell scrambled on all fours for the immediate safety of the tunnel entrance.

Somehow spared, the helicopter lifted and dashed toward the eastern horizon, a dying shrill and fading wink of navigation lights beyond harm's reach.

The night was icy against a film of sweat that shone on Durell's fevered cheeks. He held the Beretta out, slipped inside the tunnel, flattened himself against the rough stone wall. A moment passed as he waited with suppressed breath. There was a scent of guano, a cold aura of violence.

When nothing happened, he thumbed the light.

Dara lay on her back, her smudged linen skirt askew around her long thighs.

Her temple was streaked with blood.

He shook her. "Dara?" He swung the light into the chapel area, saw no one.

A moan escaped her delicate lips as he probed the wound. A bullet had creased her scalp. He thought she would be all right. She must have come in here and stumbled on McNamara—or perhaps followed him and got the worst of it. But why wasn't McNamara still here, waiting for him?

Durell could not wait for Dara to revive, and he could not leave her to Prince Tahir's mercy. He must try to carry her. Balancing on his good leg, he hoisted her onto his shoulder and limped toward the rear of the tunnel, beyond the chapel. She was not a small woman, and the strain was tremendous in his weakened condition.

An opening behind the chapel's altar took him into a refectory with table and benches carved from the stone, then into a soot-encrusted kitchen with baking ovens, fireplaces, and storage pits for wines and fats that must have been last used centuries ago. He stepped carefully around a shallow pit where monks had trampled grapes and a vat into which the juice had flowed.

He kept going, his breath sounding in hard bursts against the eerie silence. The tunnel descended abruptly, and he almost lost his footing. Dara stirred on his shoulder, moaned. He stopped, sat her against a wall.

"It's me," he said. He held her cheeks between thumb and forefinger. Her lips were slack and a sprinkling of small freckles stood out on her wan cheeks.

He slapped her, not too hard.

Her eyes opened; a light of recognition came into her irises when she saw Durell. "Oh, what a headache," she breathed.

"I should have known better than to trust you."

"You didn't. Not really. You just used me. I wasn't supposed to get here first, was I?"

"Can you walk?"

She rose, steadied herself against the wall. "I'm a bit wobbly. Where's McNamara?"

"Ahead, somewhere. We're under the hill, trying to catch up. What happened?"

Dara shook her head to clear her mind, and her short, golden hair shimmered in the light of his electric torch. "I saw you come out of here and head for the house," she said. "I thought you might have Princess Ayla hidden here—"

"So you came to kill her," Durell supplied.

"I didn't want to." She hung her head. "It was the only way to put an end to the threat, once and for all." She looked about, dejection showing on her face. "Apparently McNamara arrived at the same moment I did. The princess ran—down in here, somewhere. He must have followed her."

"You're lucky to be alive."

She leaned against him. Her heartbeat came through his shirtfront, strong and frightened. "Oh, Sam—I'm so glad you're here. I'll follow orders, I promise."

The sounds of Tahir's men came from the cave's upper reaches. Durell handed her pistol to her. "Come on," he said.

They followed the tunnel past a turning and came upon a big stone disc that stood on edge in a slot in the wall. Durell ran his hands over its rim, testing for a grip.

"What is that?" Dara asked.

"A door of sorts. Let's see if we can roll it across the tunnel behind us." He heaved with Dara's help, but he could not get much thrust from his bad leg, and the thick wheel refused to budge.

He heard footsteps, voices. "Forget it," he said.

They turned into an endless series of descending burrows. He kept his Beretta in a loose, ready grasp. The tunnel leveled, widened, became a series of living quarters, kitchens, storage bins. Tight crawlways spanned out everywhere, linking one complex to the next. The place smelled of damp and dust, nothing human.

He had heard of such underground cities, begun as early as the Second and Third Centuries, when early Christians fled to the barren Melendiz hills to avoid persecution by pagan Romans. They had been enlarged through the ages and eventually held thousands of villagers in safety when invaders razed the countryside. In places they were seven layers deep and extended for miles.

Whether by design or intuition, Princess Ayla had chosen well when she came to hide at the house of Dr. Köse. If danger threatened, she could flee to these caves just as the villagers of old had done.

He wondered if they would ever find her.

As he moved further into the mute complex, he was awed and somewhat apprehensive. It would be easy to become hopelessly lost down here, or fall into one of the wind shafts that kept the air so remarkably fresh.

He considered the lead that McNamara had and decided the man could not be far ahead. But then Tahir was not far behind.

At that moment the strained tones of a woman's voice echoed from an opening on the right.

Princess Ayla.

McNamara's reply came back, a harsh rebuttal, to judge by the inflection. Durell could not make it out. Quickly, he slid into the tunnel from which the sounds had come. His eyes found the wavering glow of a flashlight's reflection on pale stone. He stopped Dara with an outthrust hand.

McNamara's voice came again. "You blew everything. And you could have had it all, if you'd had the guts to take it."

Princess Ayla's voice quavered: "I couldn't go through with it. I—I couldn't."

Durell felt Dara's fingernails sink into his bicep, heard her angry whisper. "So. She was in on the plot. And you shielded her!"

"Just listen for a minute," he hissed. He crept closer.

McNamara was speaking now. "You ran out on us. Now your father has double-crossed me, and the only thing for me to do is go back with Sheik Zeid as if nothing had happened." He paused and added: "But I can't leave you alive to tell him how I was on Tahir's side. You understand that, don't you?"

"If you kill me, Sheik Zeid will know anyway," Princess Ayla retorted.

"You're wrong. The Israeli dame will take that rap—she's dead, so she can't very well deny it."

A sob. "Please. . . ."

"We could have had a really good thing."

"Don't. . . ."

Durell slipped into the room and faced McNamara. "Hold it."

McNamara froze and, by the light of his torch, took in Durell and the Beretta leveled at him. The glow of the flashlights clashed, filled the room with cold, white radiance, etched shadows in the grainy walls. McNamara was only a vague form as Durell stared above his beam. To one side, Princess Ayla was stiff and gleaming, fingers over her lips. Durell had the advantage. McNamara's body was turned toward her.

There was a note of despair in McNamara's voice as he said: "You heard."

"Everything."

A second passed.

Then McNamara's chopped .45 jerked toward Durell. Durell squeezed his trigger twice, the double blast shaking the chamber with ear-splitting thunder. The first shot went low and whacked into McNamara's gut, and he made a fish mouth, his flashlight wheeling away. His knees buckled and banged together as the second slug penetrated breastbone, heart, and spine. He was dead when he hit the floor.

There was a moment of startled silence.

The acrid odor of gunsmoke brushed Durell's nostrils.

Then another voice came from behind. Durell did not catch its meaning, but saw Princess Ayla's eyes widen and heard her gasp with relief.

"Father!" she cried.

"Thank you for disposing of this pig," Prince Tahir said. "He was to have died with Sheik Zeid, but he escaped. He was clever. Quite competent."

"Why did you turn on him?" Durell asked.

"He had outlived his usefulness—as I'm afraid you all have, except for my lovely daughter. Come here, my dear."

Princess Ayla went to her father, a stunned, groggy look in her black eyes. The violence around her seemed beyond her comprehension, and Durell could not guess how she had become involved in Prince Tahir's bloody scheme, unless he had forced her.

Only two of the prince's men were with him, but they were armed with M–16s. The rest must be scattered through the maze of tunnels, Durell decided. There were only a handful of them in any case.

"You will drop your weapons, please." Tahir's voice

was composed and elegant now. Much of the tension seemed to have gone out of him. Durell and Dara had no choice but to do as he commanded.

Princess Ayla watched wide-eyed, speechless.

Durell spoke. "The emir is free. Your plot is a shambles."

Prince Tahir snorted and said: "On the contrary. General Abdurrahman's troops are en route to Dhubar at this moment—and the worthy sheik has a long distance to go before he can arrive there alive." His twisted mouth smiled. "I will wager he does not make it. Matters still will work out, despite my stupid daughter."

"There will be war if the Turks invade Dhubar." It was Dara. Her eyes flamed with a fanaticism Durell had never before seen.

"Father . . . ?" Princess Ayla lifted a beseeching face to Prince Tahir.

"Hush, my child."

A long moment passed, as Tahir's eyes switched from Durell to Dara and back, and his narrow face seemed to lengthen and harden. Something squeaked: it could have been a bat or a shoe, back in the tunnels. McNamara's body lay grotesque on the floor, twisted awkwardly, as if life had been wrung from him like water from a cloth.

Everybody knew what was coming—that Prince Tahir was about to order the two soldiers to fire. Durell tasted copper, felt the cold weight of Dara's hand slide into his.

The dank air was charged with onrushing violence.

"Father, I beg you, no more killing!" Princess Ayla cried.

The back of Prince Tahir's hand slapped across her cheek, and she crashed to the floor. Her eyes widened with shock and hurt.

"You must not interfere, my dear!" Tahir screeched. "I told you: all will be well."

"Not for you, my prince," another voice said.

All heads turned and found Sheik Zeid standing in the mouth of a dark side tunnel. The flesh around one eye was puffed and bruised, and he held an M–16 evidently taken from one of Tahir's men. His sensitive eyes slid lovingly toward Princess Ayla. "I couldn't go away and leave you." And then, to Durell: "When I circled back, there was no one to stop me. All of Prince Tahir's men must have been underground."

An abrupt sound of anguish escaped Princess Ayla's lips, and she flung herself into Sheik Zeid's arms.

Durell shouted for her to get out of his way, but it was too late. In the instant that she blocked Sheik Zeid's line of fire, the quicker of Tahir's two soldiers whipped his rifle toward him. Durell took the chance, dove for the soldier, hammered the hard edge of his palm into his neck, and heard a vertebra crack.

Flashlights fell.

There was a deafening chatter as someone's rifle went off, and dust and stone chips spewed from the ceiling.

Dara grappled with the second soldier, and Durell spun to help her, felt a rip of pain in his thigh, and went down on a buckling leg. Another soldier appeared from somewhere, leapt on his chest.

Everything was confused.

The room was an amber cage of flashing shadows.

Sheik Zeid was helping Dara. Through flailing fists Durell saw Tahir throw a forearm around Princess Ayla's throat and drag her brutally into a tunnel, holding her as a shield. Her mouth worked with screams, whether from hysterics or fear of her father he did not know. Gasps, thumps, and cries filled the gleaming air as Durell and his opponent locked together in deadly embrace, breaths gushing, fingers clawing and stabbing. The man's mouth blew an odor of stale onions. He reared back and raised a rifle butt to crush Durell's skull. Durell heaved, rolled, and had the soldier beneath him. He got the steel rifle barrel across the other's windpipe and put all his weight on it. There was a throaty sound of squeezed air, a drumming of heels as clenched teeth showed and eyes bulged.

The man went limp.

Wearily, Durell looked to his left just in time to see Dara break away from Sheik Zeid and the man with whom he struggled. Murder was in her eyes as she dipped to retrieve a fallen pistol and ran into the tunnel after Princess Ayla and her father.

"Dara!" he shouted.

She did not look back.

"Don't shoot her!" he yelled.

He got up, took a step, and his leg went out from under him. It had no more strength than a soda straw. His fingers touched the fallen Beretta, wrapped around it, and he was distracted by a thick grunt. He twisted, saw Sheik Zeid unconscious beneath the pummeling fists of the Turk soldier. The Beretta kicked in his hand, and the soldier flipped onto his back.

Durell got up and fell once more.

"Dara-a-h!" His voice rippled down the tunnel and came back tauntingly. His leg had carried him as far as it would go.

His mind dim with pain and fatigue, he went on hands and knees to Sheik Zeid, checked him over, decided his injury wasn't likely to be serious. Urgently he tried to awaken him so that the emir might catch Dara before it was too late. But it was hopeless for the moment.

All he could do was start crawling.

He spared a thought for the remainder of Prince Tahir's men. Two or three might be left, but he could not let that make a difference. The small chamber smelled of gunsmoke and death as he hefted a flashlight and entered the tunnel.

He had not gone far when a high scream of terror pierced the damp silence. He checked himself as it trailed away despairingly.

Whose voice that was, he could not have said, but there seemed no point to going on, regardless. If it had been Dara, he could never stop Prince Tahir; and if it had been Princess Ayla, it was too late to stop Dara.

He leaned against the wall, guts cramped with anxiety, and tried to gather his strength.

About a minute passed, and then he heard sobs. As the sounds came closer, he thumbed his torch and picked out Dara. Weeping against her shoulder as they walked arm in arm was Princess Ayla.

Durell heaved a long sigh of relief and spoke to Dara. "What made you change your mind?"

Dara smoothed the tormented princess' shining black hair. "She is no enemy of ours or Sheik Zeid's," she said. "She deliberately led her father into an air shaft. Tahir is dead."

Chapter 23

"There they go, the princess and her prince," Dara said as a sleek executive jet bore Sheik Zeid and the Thirteenth Princess away from the provincial capital of Kayseri.

Durell's eyes followed the jet until it was a speck above the southern mountains. He swung his wheelchair awkwardly and irritably away from the window of the VIP lounge where he and Dara awaited separate flights.

"Don't get teary over it," he said.

"Well, I can't help it, Sam. One becomes hardened in our business. Seeing the sort of love they have makes me feel a little more human myself." She took a chair beside him, crossed her lovely legs, and blew her nose prettily. It was only a few hours ago that Sheik Zeid, battered somewhat but little the worse for wear, had flown them out of the weird valley of fairy chimneys, but there had been time for showers, food, even a bit of rest after initial formalities with Turkish Security. In a new traveling suit of simple design, Dara looked as wholesome as a spring flower. She had resiliency in abundance.

Durell wasn't so sure about himself. He felt worn to the nub, maybe because of the injured leg stretched out before him. It hurt like hell, but he had no intention of drugging himself with the painkillers prescribed by a Turkish physician.

He preferred to keep his senses sharp.

There were plenty of old enemies as well as new.

The doctor had ordered hospitalization for treatment of the leg, but Durell had refused. He could not really rest until he had filed his reports, although he had made a phone call to the embassy in Ankara giving the gist of his mission's conclusion.

"I do wish them a nice life in Dhubar," Dara said. "Do you think they have a chance, after all this?" She was still thinking of Zeid and Ayla.

"I suppose the people will give them the benefit of the doubt, now that McNamara isn't there to stir up the crowds," Durell said.

"He was behind the whole thing, wasn't he?"

"In the beginning, yes. But it got out of his control. He was merely supposed to check out the families of the sheik's prospective brides through his intelligence sources. Evidently he arranged for unfavorable reports while searching for someone amenable to his plan. Then he found Prince Tahir, and they worked out the whole scheme for a takeover, even to Pat's fomenting the 'foreign-inspired' riots as a pretext for calling on Turkish protection."

Dara sighed. "He could see the billions of dollars in oil revenues rolling into Dhubar. It must have driven him crazy to be so tantalizingly close to such wealth."

"All he wanted was to milk the treasury," Durell agreed. "Of course, he had learned of my mission through his contacts in Washington, and he tried to wipe me in London. He knew of the safe house in Istanbul through his past K Section affiliation and sent Prince's Tahir's men there after killing Volkan to keep him from talking—he was never in any danger in the cistern. He played it cozy the whole way, always keeping a veneer of legitimacy just in case things turned sour—as they did, finally."

Dara said, "He didn't know that Prince Tahir had bigger ideas."

"Like the restoration of the Ottoman Empire," Durell

supplied. "He didn't realize the prince would have no further use for him, once assured of Dhubar's regency for Princess Ayla. Prince Tahir didn't turn on him until he had delivered the document of regency, entrusted to him by Sheik Zeid. Saved there, all McNamara could do was kill Princess Ayla so that she could never tell how he had plotted against Sheik Zeid."

"But why did Prince Tahir take the document to General Abdurrahman?" Dara wondered.

"Possibly as proof that everything had been arranged so that he could move on Dhubar," Durell conjectured. "The old emir's assassin must have been one of Abdurrahman's men. Tracing him into the Turkish military zone of Cyprus would have been nearly impossible." Durell gently massaged his cramping leg and added, "General Abdurrahman will be arrested aboard his command ship today, I'm told."

"I still can't believe that Princess Ayla plotted against the man she loved so much," Dara said.

"That was the catch," Durell said. "She was totally under her father's influence and just as calculating as he, at first. The trouble was, she fell in love. She must have fought the emotion, because she even persuaded Zeid to sign the document of regency after the baby was born."

"I suppose he thought of that as no more than reasonable to insure the succession of his son," Dara said.

"It was really his death warrant," Durell said. "Under the dominance of her father, Princess Ayla went along—until the assassination of the old emir. He was ill and frail, and she had thought he would be allowed to die a natural death. She couldn't handle the violence—she knew then she could not go through with the murder of her husband. She returned to Dhubar determined to save him. But then she realized she could do that only by exposing her father's treachery."

"That was when she called on your help, at the mosque in Dhubar," Dara said.

"She was panic-stricken. She didn't wait to see me; she just ran away. She left Tahir as much in the lurch as us."

"She knew her father could do nothing without her, so

the only way to save her husband was to give him up," Dara said.

"If Nadine hadn't acted on her intuition, it might have ended quite differently," Durell said. "Prince Tahir was certain to find his daughter sooner or later. And he might have convinced her she was in too deep to turn back."

"Didn't Sheik Zeid say Nadine would live with them in Dhubar now?"

Durell nodded. "As soon as she is able to travel. She had a concussion and bruised ribs, but the injuries shouldn't hold her up long. Sheik Zeid owes her a lot."

A sentimental moisture glistened again in Dara's eyes. "There will be a grand time in the old palace tonight, now that he has forgiven Princess Ayla," she said.

"Forgiven? He practically threw himself at her feet."

"Oh, damn." Dara dug for her handkerchief again. "I still say it's beautiful."

"Maybe—if Princess Ayla has learned her lesson. She still stands to be regent if anything happens to the emir," Durell replied.

"You're a cynic, Samuel Cullen Durell."

"It helps in my line of work."

The public-address system echoed through the small terminal, calling Dara's flight. She took Durell's hand. "We've shared so much, Sam. I don't want to go to Jerusalem just yet."

"You must," Durell said. "I'll be in Antalya. They say the Mediterranean air performs wonders of healing this time of year."

"In two days, then?"

"I'll wait for you, if I can."

"It's too bad about McNamara," General Dickinson McFee told Durell. "He was a good man, once."

"Good at playing both sides," Durell replied.

"The boys on the Mideast desk will miss him. They feel as if they've had an eye put out."

"They'll grow another."

The deceptively innocent-looking little chief of K Section sipped his sparkling *tonik*. Even in the shade of the hotel garden it was hot, here on Turkey's southern coast. But McFee, dressed in a gray, tropical-weight suit, looked perfectly cool. The routine reports had not sufficed for the mission of the Thirteenth Princess, and the boss had met Durell in the seventeen-hundred-year-old resort of Antalya to debrief him personally. Now they were saying goodbye.

McFee broke the breezy silence. "At least our oil supply is assured for a few more years."

"Or months," Durell said.

"Don't be gloomy, Samuel. Relax and take what satisfaction you can. You did your job well."

Durell toyed with his bourbon and soda. The wheelchair annoyed him almost beyond endurance, but the medical men had absolutely forbidden him to walk for another day or so. It seemed he had come frightfully close to losing a leg. The lovely town pleasured his senses, its white buildings scattered amid flowers and trees down to a small yacht harbor with green, red, and blue boats. The crescent of Konyaalti beach swept away to the Lycian Mountains in the west.

But Durell's dark blue eyes showed no pleasure with McFee as he said: "There was more than courtesy involved in linking me with Israeli intelligence on this, wasn't there, sir?"

McFee looked briefly uncomfortable. "I see no point in going into that," he said.

"Dara had orders to kill Princess Ayla from the start, didn't she?"

"Only if you dropped the ball. It was preferable that you get her out of the country. That had first priority. Miss Allon's experience suited her admirably to back you up if you failed." He took a short breath. "We could hardly allow a calamity in Dhubar, if the sacrifice of Princess Ayla's life would have prevented it," he said in a reasoning tone. "We couldn't have an American involved in that, of course. There would have been disastrous complications with Sheik Zeid, if he'd found out."

Durell's tone did not soften. "So I was put in the

position of trying to save her from my own eager colleague."

"I regret that, Samuel."

"You regret?"

"Deeply." After a momentary pause, McFee switched the subject. "When may I expect you back in Washington?"

"Not soon."

"Your doctor says—"

Durell cut him off. "It is not the doctor's leg."

He ignored McFee's reaction, whatever it might be, and looked out at sparkling Vs cut by pleasure launches in the flat sea. He scented the soft and languorous fragrance of the water, admired the uncrowded beach.

Then he turned his gaze to McFee and said: "I'll need a month, at least." He raised a palm at the man's pale, bickering eyes. "I regret it," he said.

McFee studied his face for several seconds, then rose from his chair. "Two weeks. No more," he said.

And he walked away.

Durell stayed at the shaded table and enjoyed his drink as the sea breeze cooled his bruised face and teased his hair. Shortly, he felt hands on the grips of his wheelchair.

"Shall I push you around a bit?" Dara smiled down over his shoulder.

"Sorry. It might get to be a habit."

"How did it go?"

"I got the two weeks, same as you."

He swung out of the chair and put his weight gingerly on the injured leg. It didn't feel so bad.

"Sam! You're not supposed to do that."

He smiled, for the first time in days, it seemed, as he admired the soft and inviting forms her body took in its long descent from neck to ankle. Her perfume mixed the air with a light, summery scent.

"There's lots I'm not supposed to do yet," he said, and guided her away from the table, an arm about her waist. He looked down at her eager eyes and added: "But now that you're here, let's do them all."

Edward S. Aarons
"Assignment Series"